OUTLAW JUSTICE

ROBERT VAUGHAN

WOLFPACK
PUBLISHING
— EST 2013 —

WOLFPACK
PUBLISHING
— EST 2013 —

The characters and events portrayed in this book are
fictitious. Any similarity to real persons, living or dead, is
coincidental and not intended by the author.

Published by Wolfpack Publishing
5130 S. Fort Apache Road, 215-380
Las Vegas, NV 89148

Paperback IBSN 978-1-64734-356-9
eBook ISBN 978-1-64734-355-2

OUTLAW JUSTICE

CHAPTER ONE

A large green Concord stage, with yellow letters proudly proclaiming the carrier, Wells Fargo, came rolling into the Oak Grove way station, at nine o'clock on a cold night. The coach was pulled by six prancing horses blowing fog in the cold night air, and driven by Emmet Dobson, who wearily pulled the big team to a halt. It had left Eugene City at two o'clock in the afternoon, and was scheduled to reach Ashland, its destination, before nightfall the next day. Oak Grove was one of twelve stations that marked the 180 miles that separated the two points.

"Looks like it's fixin' to rain," Dobson said.

"It's Oregon, what do you expect?" Troy Elliot, his shotgun messenger replied.

There were six passengers on board, four men and two women, and they left the stage exhausted and grateful for the sparse comfort offered by the way station for the night. Their luggage remained in the tightly lashed leather boot, where it would remain dry and secure despite the impending rain. The window curtains, however, would do little to keep out the rain, so that tomorrow morning the passengers would resume the trip on hard leather seats that were cold and wet.

"Will you be comin' in, Troy, or will you be sleepin' in the barn?" Emmet asked.

"These places offer only one bed to the driver and shotgun messenger."

"How do you know? This is your first trip; you've never been to Oak Grove before."

"They're all alike," Troy replied.

The horses were taken out of harness and led into the barn just before the rain started. Troy, who carried a blanket for such a purpose, made himself a bed of straw, then curled up in his blanket.

It was no surprise that Wells Fargo had hired Troy Elliot to ride as shotgun guard for them. He was the best man with a gun anyone in the Wells Fargo system had ever seen, and though he was only twenty-three, and looked even younger. He was a man who had the respect of all who knew him.

Troy had not set out to become a gunfighter. His boyhood ambition had been to go to sea, for that had been the way of his grandfather. Troy could still remember the marvelous stories of wondrous far-off places that he had heard at his grandfather's knee. But his grandfather died when Troy was fourteen, and Troy's father and mother, younger sister, and Troy himself moved west where his father opened a general merchandise store.

As Troy lay warm in the barn, listening to the sound of the rain, the memories came back to him. By the time he was sixteen, Troy had come to enjoy the great West though he had not yet given up his dream of going to sea. But all his hopes and dreams ended in one night of horror. It was a night that Troy would never allow himself to forget.

Seven years earlier:

Troy's family lived in three rooms behind his father's store. They had just started supper one night when the bell on the front door rang as it was pushed open.

"I thought I locked the front door," his father had said in surprise. He glanced at the clock on the wall. "It's way too late for any normal customer. I wonder who it is."

"Shall I see, Pop?" Troy asked.

"No, I'll go," James Elliot said. He stood up but had no sooner gained his feet than their small apartment was invaded by four men.

"Just sit down, Pops," one of the men said. "We'll serve ourselves." The man who spoke was a big man, with a scar twisting his face into grotesque ugliness. He walked over to the table and grabbed a piece of meat from the platter. "This looks good," he said.

"What is this?" James demanded angrily. "Who are you? What do you want?"

"Who I am don't make no never mind," the man said, tearing into the meat with yellowed teeth. "I want some supplies."

"Well, this is not the way to go about it. Come back tomorrow when the store is open."

"We can't do that, Pops," the man said. "You see, we robbed us a bank earlier today, and we got us a posse on our tails. Right now, we need some ammunition and some grub to take with us. We gotta hide out for a while."

"Get out of this store right now!" Troy's father demanded, pushing the scar faced man away from the table.

The man simply pulled his gun and shot Jim Elliot dead, without so much as a second thought.

"James!" Troy's mother screamed, running to her husband's body.

"Well, Deke, lookie here what we got," one of the others said, looking at Troy's mother. "Are you think'n what I'm thinkin'? Get Grady in here."

"You get away from her!" Troy shouted. He grabbed the meat knife from the table and started toward his mother's assailant, but before he could get to him, he heard the loud noise of a pistol shot, and felt a burning, breathtaking pain as the bullet slammed into his back. He fell to the floor, unable to move.

"What do you say, Boss?" the one called Deke said when another man entered the room. "We got a couple o' women here, well, one of 'em is pretty young, but I like 'em young. Why don't we have a little fun with 'im?"

"No," the newcomer said. "We must leave at once. That is, unless you wish to see the posse descending upon us through the front door."

This man's voice, unlike the others, was cultured and educated.

"I reckon he's right," one of the men said. "Come on, let's go."

"What'll we do with 'em?"

"Grady, let's burn the store, that'll take care of 'em, don't you think?"

"Don't be a fool," Grady said. "If you set a torch to this place, they'll see it burning for twenty miles. You might as well just ride into the posse with your hands up."

"Well, whatta you think we should do?"

"Kill them," the cultured voice said.

"The man and the boy are already dead," one of the others said. "You wanna kill the women too?"

"We have no choice now."

"I don't know, I don't hold much with killin' no women."

"You get the supplies loaded onto the horses. I'll do

what must be done."

Troy tried with all his might to move to reach the knife which lay just in front of his outstretched fingers, but he couldn't. He lay there, in horror, as the one called Grady calmly shot first his mother and then his sister.

Grady had not come in until after Troy was shot. Because of that, Troy was unable to see his face, but he did notice his hands. The fingers were long and delicate looking, almost like a woman's. That wasn't much to help him identify someone, but it was all he had to go on. That, and the cultured, educated voice. Troy lay there, grieved by the loss of his family, and determined to find justice.

Customers found Troy the next day, and they took him to the doctor's office. The doctor removed the bullet which was causing pressure on his spine, and after the bullet was removed, the paralysis which had overtaken Troy was slowly relieved.

Troy was only sixteen years old, with no wish to run his father's store, so he sold it, but not before he took the finest pistol and holster, and rifle and saddle sheath that were in stock, along with a large supply of ammunition. Troy immediately began his search for the five outlaws, all the while practicing his draw, and taking part-time jobs to keep him going. By the time he was twenty, his draw was like greased lightning, and at sixty paces he could put six bullets into a silver dollar in less than three seconds.

In the seven years since that awful night, Troy had held a series of jobs. He had been a cowhand on a trail drive, he had been a civilian scout for the army, he had been a deputy sheriff, he had even made one sea voyage, in keeping with his old wish. Now he was a shotgun messenger for Welles Fargo. As the memories faded, he could hear the rain continuing to fall, and Troy's eyes grew heavy. He drifted off to sleep.

* * *

The cold rain that had begun during the night continued until morning, slashing down on the small, weather-beaten house which perched precariously on the edge of Canyon Creek Pass. The back door of the house opened then slammed shut, and someone hurried through the dark and the rain to a barn which stood some thirty yards distant from the main building.

The hurrying figure moved gracefully across the distance and slipped into the barn. Sure hands removed a match from a waxed, waterproof box to light a kerosene lantern. When the flame was turned up, a small golden bubble of light cast long shadows inside the barn, and at the same time illuminated the face of the lantern holder. It was only then that one would have noticed that it was a woman. She had hair as black as a raven's wing, and it fell softly to her shoulders from beneath the felt hat she wore.

The girl's name was Alexandria Pendleton, though if anyone had asked, she would have said her name was Alex, as that was what she preferred to be called. Alex was twenty years old, and the daughter of Rice Pendleton, a Wells Fargo stage driver and station agent for this way station, where they lived. The station was known as Oak Grove way station, and Alex helped her father run it. In fact, she often went along with him on the Oak Grove to Roseburg run, helping him drive. She had a light, sure touch on the "ribbons", as the reins were called, and played upon them, three in each hand, one rein for each horse, with the skill and virtuosity of a master violinist.

There were those who argued that such work was ill-becoming for a young woman, and they chastised Rice for the arrangement. The most vocal of these detractors was Pricilla Barnett, Alex's maternal aunt. Aunt Pricilla, who was Mrs. Tobias Barnett of the Denver Barnetts, had begun petitioning Rice to allow Alex to live with them from the moment Alex's mother had died.

"Alex likes it up here with me," Rice had insisted. "And I would miss her more than I could bear if she were to stay away too long."

"Alexandria is a lovely young woman now," Pricilla had replied. "It is only right that she get away from horses and wagons and the ruffians who abound near such places, and come to Denver to live with us. We will arrange introductions with all of the proper people, and see to it that she meets qualified young gentlemen of means."

"I'll think it over," Rice had promised, after being relentlessly bombarded by Pricilla's demands.

Alex was fully aware of the battle going on between her father and her mother's sister, but she had already resolved to stay right here regardless of the final outcome. She was born to this kind of life and she loved it. She thrilled to the sound of the stage driver's trumpet as the stage approached the station. She liked the smell of leather and cured wood, and the feel of power when she held the reins of six spirited animals. She liked to see the daily parade of passengers and guess about their backgrounds and wonder if they found life as exciting as she did.

Alex walked over to the first of the six horses that would form the hitch for the coach. She leaned against the horse and began stroking his neck.

It was warm and dry inside the barn, though the

sounds of the wind and the rain outside were testimony of the cold, wet beginning of the new day. In a way there was something sensuous about the protected isolation of the barn.

The horses moved expectantly toward the trough to await their morning meal of oats.

"Good morning, my friends," Alex said. "Did you sleep well?"

Alex began scooping oats into the trough and continued to talk to the horses as if they could understand her. In fact, Alex had such a way with horses that there were those who believed she really could speak with them.

"Listen to the rain, horses," she said to them. "Doesn't it feel good to be warm and dry inside, with the rain coming down outside?"

"It feels very good," a voice answered her.

"What?" Alex asked, gasping.

A young man suddenly sat up from the straw of one of the empty stalls, laughing. "What's the matter, miss? Did you think perhaps the horses were talking back to you?"

"Sir, you should have made your presence known!" Alex gasped.

"I'm sorry," the young man said, still laughing. "But the opportunity was too good to pass. You should have seen your face when you thought a horse had answered you."

"I did not think a horse answered me," Alex insisted.

"Oh, yes you did." The stranger brushed at the straw that was the same yellow color as his hair, until the last piece of it was removed from his clothes. He had a smooth, boyishly handsome face, but Alex was still too angered by his rude intrusion to notice.

"Who are you? Where did you come from?" Alex asked.

"My name is Troy Elliot," the young man said. "I arrived on the stage last night."

"No, you did not," Alex said. "There were only six passengers on that stage; I know that for a fact."

"Oh, ho, you're so smart," Troy teased. "But, for your information, I'm not a passenger. I'm riding as the shotgun messenger."

"Messenger? You expect me to believe Wells Fargo would hire a mere boy for shotgun guard."

For a split-second Troy's eyes lost their humor, but the humor returned as quickly as it left. "When a gun is fired, it doesn't make any difference how old the finger is that pulls the trigger."

Now it was Alex's turn to laugh. The remark about his age had a telling effect, just as she hoped it would. In her mind it had evened things up for his startling her. She decided to press her advantage further. "You are a bit touchy over your age, aren't you? But then, boys always are."

CHAPTER TWO

Troy didn't know why he had let the young woman's dismissive comment about his age get under his skin. But even as he thought that, he knew exactly why. It was because she was a woman. He didn't know whether it was a blessing or a curse that he looked younger than his years, but as he had told her in a pique, when a gun is fired, it doesn't make any difference how old the finger is that pulls the trigger.

That theory had already been put to the test.

Troy had been sixteen years old when his family was murdered, and he was left for dead. It was three years later, when he encountered the first two of the men who had visited the store on that awful day. Though he recognized both of them, he knew only that one was called Deke Jenkins. They were drinking at a bar when he saw them.

"You, Jenkins, I've been looking for you, and that even uglier son of a bitch standing there beside you, for a very long time and now I've found you," Troy said.

"What?" Jenkins replied, confused as to why a mere boy would have the nerve to challenge them, for Troy's face was that of a youth much younger than his nineteen years. "Who the hell are you? Are you even old enough to be in a saloon?"

"My name is Troy Elliot. Does that name mean anything to you?"

The two men looked at each other with insolent grins on their faces. "Naw, kid, that don't mean nothin'," Deke said. "Is it supposed to?"

Perhaps if I showed you the bullet scar in my back, it would remind you of the time you murdered my father, mother, and sister, shot me in the back and left me for dead. Would you remember that?" Troy asked.

His voice was calm, and soft with the inflection of youth. But his words fell like ice with the impact of their meaning.

The others at the bar backed away then, leaving the youth and the two villains facing one another. Slowly the two men spread apart, putting distance between them, making it difficult for Troy to cover them both.

"I thought you was dead," Deke said easily.

"I recovered."

"Maybe you wasn't hurt all that bad in the first place. Maybe you was just too scared to do anythin' about it," the other desperado said.

"I'm going to ask you two men, nicely, to drop your gun belts and come to the sheriff's office with me," Troy said.

"Haw, lissen to that!" Jenkins laughed. "Kid, if you know what's good for you, you'll hightail it on outta here 'afore we finish the job we started five years ago."

"I'm taking you in, dead or alive," Troy said.

"Boy, you're talkin' like you think you're pretty good with that hog leg," Jenkins said, pointing to the pistol hanging at Troy's side. "But no matter how good you are, you can't shoot but one of us, 'n the other'n 's gonna get you."

"Suppose we put it to a test," Troy said calmly.

"Dammit, Deke, this boy aims to kill us both!" the other man suddenly said. "Let's take our chances with the sheriff."

"No!" Jenkins shouted to his partner. "Fill your hand, you cowardly son of a bitch!"

As Jenkins called out, his gun started coming up from the sheath he wore tied down on his side. Before his gun had even cleared his holster, Troy's gun boomed and bucked in his hand, and Deke grabbed at the hole in his chest with a look of surprise on his face. Then, through the blue puff of smoke, Troy's gun barked a second time, and the other man fell, firing his gun ineffectively into the floor as he did so.

The smoke from the three discharges hung over the barroom, and its acrid smell burned the eyes and throats of the patrons, but when it rolled away there was the smooth-skinned, clear-eyed youth standing calmly, with his gun once again sheathed, looking at the bodies of the two men he had shot.

Even as everyone was standing around in shock, staring at the two bodies lying on the floor, the sheriff arrived.

"What's going on here?" he asked.

Everyone began talking at once but finally he was able to put together the story that Troy had shot the two men when they drew on him.

"I'll be damn," the sheriff said. "That's Deke Jenkins, and Felix Doran. There's a two-hundred-fifty-dollar bounty on each one of 'em. Is that what you are, boy? A bounty hunter?"

"No, but I'll take the reward."

Troy's reputation began with that confrontation, and it grew when two of the remaining three tracked him down.

Both men fancied themselves fast with a gun, and indeed, they were known and feared throughout the West as gunfighters. Neither had any intention of fleeing from a mere boy. And though each thought he was able to handle Troy alone, they wanted to take no chances, so they faced him together. They found him in a small California town and called him out into the street.

There were perhaps a hundred people along the sidewalks and in the buildings, looking out at the scene. The gun-wise veterans of the outlaw trail, who had perhaps a score of killings between them, drew first, and one of their bullets carried away Troy's hat, while the other burned a painful but not serious brand across his arm. Troy fired only twice, and both his missiles found their mark in the outlaws' hearts.

Now there remained only the mysterious Grady. Grady, with the woman's hands and the cultured talk, who was forewarned that Troy lived and was looking for him. And to make matters more difficult, Troy's reputation was preceding him wherever he went. That meant that Grady would know Troy before Troy recognized him. But that didn't deter Troy from his efforts to find him. It was while he was searching for Grady and taking jobs where he found them that he wound up in the barn of Oak Grove stagecoach way station on this rainy morning.

The coffee Alex Pendleton had started just before going to feed the horses was done, and its rich aroma filled the kitchen. Her father, who would be taking the stage on to Wolf Creek, and Russell Wood, the driver who had brought it in from Eugene City, were already in the kitchen and they leaned against the sideboard, drinking the coffee they had poured for themselves.

"Did ya feed the horses?" Rice Pendleton asked.

"Yes," Alex answered. She opened the oven and tried to remove the pan of biscuits, but she was so angry that she forgot to use a pot holder. As a result, she burned her hand, and dropped the biscuits on the table with a shout of pain.

"Honey, it ought not to take too many times to learn that a biscuit pan is hot when it first comes out of the oven," Rice teased.

"It wasn't hot. It just didn't take her long to look at it," Russell said, then he laughed uproariously at his own joke. Finally, both men quit laughing when they saw that Alex wasn't appreciating their humor.

"Did you see Troy out there?" Russell asked.

"I saw him," Alex answered shortly.

"Is he awake?"

"Yes."

"Then I reckon he'll be in for breakfast without my havin' to go through the rain to fetch 'im."

"Say, who is this fella, this Troy?" Rice asked. Rice was sliding on waterproof overalls to help fight off the rain, since he would be driving while exposed to the elements.

"His name is Troy Elliot," Russell said. "He'll be ridin' as the shotgun messenger for you."

"Troy Elliot? Haven't I heard that name?"

"I should think you have," Russell said. "He's the fella that shot them two yahoos down in California last year. You might'a heard of them two: Sol Cook and Lance Holman."

"Gunfighters, weren't they?"

"I doubt that there were ever two meaner hombres that walked like men," Russell said. "Anyhow, the story is, they called the boy down, and he faced 'em square n proper, then kilt 'em both."

"At the same time?"

"Yep."

"He must be fast."

"Faster'n anyone I ever saw. I can tell you that for sure. You can tell by lookin' at 'im. I mean the way he carries hisself 'n all."

At that moment, the young man who was the object of their conversation came in through the back door, then shook the rainwater from the crown of his hat. He stood there looking around, poised, Alex thought, like a cat, light on his feet, ready to spring.

"Would you like some coffee?" Alex asked, looking at him curiously in the light of Russell's story. Despite what Russell had said, she didn't think he had the look of a killer.

"I sure would like some," Troy answered. "And maybe a biscuit and some of that salt meat."

"I'll have some eggs in a moment," Alex said.

"This'll do, thank you," Troy said, helping himself to the fare. He pulled a chair into the corner, then tipped it back and held his coffee in one hand and the biscuit sandwich in the other. His rain slicker, Alex noticed, was flipped back out of the way, leaving the butt of his pistol exposed. Alex looked at the pistol handle but didn't see any notches carved in it. She had read somewhere that gunfighters did that to the handles of their pistols, and now she wondered if the story Russell had told them was true.

"They don't usually send a shotgun guard on this run," Rice observed.

"You don't usually carry as much as ten thousand dollars," Russell offered.

"Ten thousand dollars?" Rice whistled. "What are we doing with so much money?"

"Wells Fargo is transferin' some funds to the new branch bank in Canyonville," Russell replied. He finished his coffee and put the cup down. "Well, if you're ready we can go hitch up the team."

"Alex, honey, if you'll make me up a couple of those sandwiches there, I'll eat 'em after I get underway," Rice said.

"Are you sure you don't want to wait just a minute before you go out there?" Alex asked. "I can have your eggs in just a second."

In fact, Alex was trying to prevent them from leaving her alone with Troy, but she knew she couldn't say anything without bringing on unwanted questions.

"No, darlin', the sandwiches will be fine," Rice insisted. He and Russell pushed the door open and stepped out into the rain.

Troy remained in the kitchen with Alex. It was strangely quiet, with only the popping noise of the meat frying in the pan, the slurping noises of Troy drinking his coffee, and the seemingly louder than usual ticking of the wall clock. The clock indicated five minutes until five.

"I could not think much of a person who would take pride in murder."

The smile left Troy's face. "It wasn't murder, Miss Pendleton," he said. "I gave them a chance to surrender, and they chose to go for their guns instead. I feel no pride in what I did, but I take no shame either, for if ever there were men who deserved to die, it was those men."

"What did they do?"

"They murdered my father, my mother and my sister," Troy said.

"Oh," Alex gasped. "I...I'm sorry. I hadn't heard the reason."

"What did you hear? That I faced them down in the street, like some sort of contest?" Troy asked.

"Well, yes, as a matter of fact."

"Unfortunately, that's the part of the story that is spread around," Troy said. "And now I find that I must spend all my time avoiding such confrontations. Until I find the last one."

"The last one?"

"Yes. There's one man remaining," Troy said. "And I'll not rest until I've located him."

"Are you going to kill him, too?"

"Or bring him to justice."

She looked at the clock. "Oh, I'd better start the passengers' eggs. Would you wake them, please?"

"I'll be glad to," Troy said.

As Alex scrambled the eggs, she looked through the door and into the dark shadows of the great common room where the passengers having gotten out of bed, were now stretched out in various chairs, napping as they awaited breakfast. She could see Troy moving through the gloom, waking them gently. He moved with an easy grace and confidence.

As Alex served breakfast to the passengers, she listened to them talk. As she often did, she was able to put together enough information on each of them to establish their background. One of the women, young and pretty, was an army wife, traveling to Lime Point Military Reservation in California to join her husband, a lieutenant newly assigned to the army fort. The other woman was in her late forties, a spinster schoolteacher trying to find in a new location what she had been unable to find in any previous place. There was a farmer, a travel-wise drummer, an out-of-work mechanic and a lawyer named Grayson Thornbury.

Thornbury, who was about 30, had black hair and flashing dark eyes. A small, thin mustache was set above a well-formed mouth.

The front door opened, and Rice and Russell returned. Russell, who now had a rest period until nine o'clock when he would take a stage headed back north, bade Rice good-bye, then went into the driver's room to go back to sleep. Rice rubbed his hands together and looked over toward the passengers, gathered around the common table and just finishing breakfast.

"Folks, take one last mouthful, then climb aboard," he called. "We got us a lot of ground to cover."

There was some groaning and complaining but the passengers heeded Rice's instructions and filed out of the house to climb into the waiting stage. The drummer, seasoned by stage travel, hurried to the far corner of the coach to fix himself comfortably for a nap. Mr. Thornbury, after receiving permission from the ladies, lit up a cigar, and the others settled in as well as they could under the circumstances.

"Here are your sandwiches, Dad," Alex said, handing her father a package wrapped in oilcloth,

"Thanks, honey," Rice replied. "I'll see you tonight."

"And I'll be seeing you again too," Troy called down, hooking his heel over the footboard and cradling the rifle across his lap.

"Hyah, team!" Rice shouted. He swung the long whip out and snapped it over the heads of the six-horse hitch with a report nearly as loud as a pistol shot. The horses strained into their harness, the great wheels of the stage began to turn, and the coach started down the road. Alex went back into the house to retreat from the still-driving rain.

It was more than four hours later, after Russell had already left on the northbound stage, that the front door suddenly burst open and Alex saw the bedraggled form of Grayson Thornbury standing there, wild-eyed and dirty, his clothes torn and bloodied, looking for all the world like a visiting angel from hell.

"Miss Pendleton, there has been a terrible tragedy!" he cried out.

"Mr. Thornbury, what is it?" Alex asked, her voice reflecting her fright.

"We've been robbed, Miss Pendleton," Thornbury said. "The ten thousand dollars were taken. Everyone was killed."

"Every...did you say everyone was killed?" Alex asked, her voice barely audible with horror.

"Everyone," Thornbury said. "I'm sorry, girl, but your papa was the first to go."

"No!" Alex said, screaming in anguish. She sobbed in her heartbreak for several moments, then looked at Thornbury. "What about Troy Elliot?" she asked. "Couldn't he stop it?"

"Stop it, Miss Pendleton? Hell, miss, he was the one who did it!"

CHAPTER THREE

Rain was dripping in Troy's face, and he turned his head trying to get away from it. He thought perhaps he was still in the barn and he attempted to burrow down into the straw to get warm and dry, but there was no straw available. There seemed to be only hard wet wood, and he could draw scarce comfort from that.

Wait a minute! If he wasn't in the barn, where was he?

Troy opened his eyes to look around and saw that he was lying in the well of the driver's bench. But why? What was he doing sleeping on the job, and why had the stage stopped? He remembered climbing onto the stage to leave Oak Grove way station…so what was happening now?

Now Troy was fully conscious, and he could hear the rain drumming into the stage as well as feel it.

A wreck! That was it, there must have been a wreck! But no, the stage was upright and undamaged, and the horses were standing quietly in their harness, waiting patiently for the order to go ahead.

Troy pulled himself up and looked on the seat. The oilskin package with Rice Pendleton's breakfast was still there, but Pendleton was nowhere to be seen. Where the hell was he? Why had he stopped right in the middle of the road?

"Hey!" Troy called. "Anyone down in the box?" There was no answer, and Troy climbed over the edge, feeling his head reel as he did so. Once he reached the ground, he grabbed the wheel and stood there for a moment or two, fighting the wave of nausea and dizziness which nearly overtook him. He was aware of a throbbing pain in the back of his head, and he put his hand there. It came away with blood, and he felt a wound where he had obviously been struck by something. Or somebody. Though he couldn't remember anything like that. His last memory was of riding along in the shotgun seat.

Finally, the nausea and dizziness cleared enough for him to move, and he stepped back to open the door to the stage. "Folks, what's going on?" he started to say, then stopped when he saw that the stage was empty. There was no one inside, nor was there any luggage or any personal objects to indicate that anyone had even been there.

"What is this?" Troy said aloud. "What the hell is going on?" He pulled his gun from his holster and spun around, looking toward the side of the road. His skin prickled as if he were being watched, and he crouched slightly, staring through the rain into the rocks. Was someone up there watching him? Did somebody, even now, have a bead on him? Could he expect a rifle bullet to tear into his flesh at any moment?

After a few seconds the feeling passed, and Troy returned his gun to his holster, and looked once again at the empty stage. One of the horses snorted and stamped his foot, and the unexpected movement caused Troy to draw his pistol again. When he realized what it was, he holstered his pistol. He walked up to the lead horse and began stroking his head.

"I sure wish I could talk horse talk," he said. "I'd ask you just what happened here."

As Troy stroked the horse's head, his eyes caught something white among the rocks beside the road, and he walked over toward it. It was a piece of cloth, and unless he was mistaken, it had been torn from the dress of the young army wife. When Troy leaned over to pick it up, he looked down into the ravine which bordered the road, and then he saw them.

"Oh, my God," he cried, for down in the ravine, a drop of perhaps fifty feet, he saw the crumpled bodies of the passengers.

Troy returned to the stage and got a coil of rope; then, securing it to a rock, he dropped the end over the edge and climbed down to the bodies.

There were six of them: the two women, Rice, and the three male passengers. Three men? *Wait a minute*, Troy thought. *Weren't there four men?*

Yes, there were four men, he remembered. The dandy who had been talking to Alex was missing. Where was he, and how did he get away?

Troy checked each body and discovered that they had all been shot, presumably by the same people who had knocked him out. But who had done it? And why couldn't he remember anything about it?

Troy tied the rope around the first body, then climbed back up and pulled the body up after him. He worked hard for quite a while as the rain lashed against him, and eventually had all six bodies lying alongside the road. He covered them with a tarpaulin, then went over to the stage and sat there for a while, resting from the exertion and from the pain and nausea which threatened to overtake him.

The money! he thought suddenly. He climbed up on the driver's seat and looked for the strongbox, but it was gone. Of course, that was it! Someone had heard about the ten thousand dollars, and the temptation had been too great. But that was why he had been hired. He was supposed to protect the strongbox...and the passengers' lives. He swallowed a lump which had risen in his throat. He had failed them, just as he had failed his own family.

Troy heard horses approaching, and he hopped back down and ran to the side of the road, seeking cover behind a rock in case the murderers returned. He pulled his pistol and watched as the riders approached. There were seven of them, including the passenger who was missing from the stage, and Alex Pendleton.

"No, Alex, go back!" Troy called out, stepping out from behind the rock. "You shouldn't see this, it's..."

"That's him!" Thornbury shouted, pointing at Troy. "He did all of this!"

"What?" Troy asked. "What are you saying?" Troy suddenly saw six guns pointed at him, and he realized that they thought he was the murderer.

"Drop your gun belt, Elliot," one of the men said. "I know you're good, but I don't think you can shoot us all down."

"Shoot you down? Why would I want to shoot you down?" Troy asked. "Listen, I didn't do this terrible thing! I don't know what happened, but I—"

"We know what happened," the spokesman said. "We've got an eyewitness."

"An eyewitness? Who?"

"Me. I saw it all," Thornbury said. "You thought you'd killed me like the others. But after you shot them, and started for the strongbox, I sneaked up behind you and hit you over the head, then made it back for help."

"He's got a wound on his head, all right, look at that," one of the others said, pointing to the blood in Troy's hand.

"Mister, you're lyin'," Troy said.

"Then why don't you tell us your side of it? What happened?"

"I... I don't know," Troy said. "One minute I was riding along, and the next I was coming to. I found all of these people dead, down in the ravine. I pulled them up here and covered them with a canvas, then you rode up."

"Check his gun," Thornbury said. "See if it has been fired."

"Yes," Troy said. "I'll go along with that." He started to reach for it.

"You just step back," the leader of the posse said. "I'll pick it up."

Troy stepped back out of the way and watched the leader of the posse pick up his gun and sniff at the barrel. Troy looked up at Alex, hoping for sympathy from her, but she turned her head away from him, and he saw tears streaming down her face.

"You say you haven't fired this gun?" the man asked Troy.

"Not today."

"It smells to me like it's been fired." the man said.

"I plinked away at some cans a couple of days ago."

He opened the gate and looked at the cartridges inside the cylinder. "Did you reload the gun after shooting at the tin cans?"

"Of course, I did," Troy said. "You don't think I would come along as a guard with an empty gun, do you?"

"No, I wouldn't think so," the posse leader said. He flipped the cylinder out and ejected the contents onto the ground. There was an audible gasp from the others as they saw what fell: six empty shell casings.

"What?" Troy gasped, astonished at what he saw.

"That's all I need," someone said. "Let's hang the son of a bitch right here."

"There ain't no tree," one of the others noted.

"Then throw the rope over a rock."

"No!" Alex called out. "I don't want my father's killer lynched. That's too quick. I want him tried for it. I want him to think about it awhile."

"Alex, I didn't do it," Troy protested. "You've got to believe that!"

"Shut your mouth, mister, or I'll shoot you right where you stand," the posse leader said.

"How are we gonna get 'im back to town?" one of the men asked.

The leader turned in his saddle. "Well, I reckon we could tie him up, and then throw him in the stage. We've got to get these bodi…uh, people…in the stage too," he said, softening his statement for Alex's sake.

"No," Alex said. "I don't want him riding in the stage with my father's body." She swung down from her horse. "Put him on my horse. I'll drive the stage."

"You're gonna drive the stage?"

"Look at the road," Alex said. "Do any of you think you could turn the stage here?"

The men looked at the narrow road, then grunted in the negative.

"Well, I can," she said, climbing onto the seat, and holding the reins while the bodies were placed inside.

Troy's hands were bound behind his back and his empty pistol was put back in his holster, then he was helped up on Alex's horse. He looked at the girl.

"Alex, please, you must believe me!"

Alex didn't answer. Instead, she snapped the reins, then pulled the horses into a tight turn.

"Mr. Elliot," Thornbury said. "I am a lawyer."

"Why are you telling me? Or do you intend to represent me?"

"No," Thornbury said. "I intend to apply for permission to act as prosecutor in this case. I am going to enjoy watching you hang by the neck until your demise, Mr. Elliot."

"Demise, listen to that purty word," one of the men said, laughing. "I tell you, Grayson, you're so educated you make dyin' sound almost dignified."

"Lookit that, the girl's got the stage turned. I don't think her daddy could'a done a better job on it. Come on, let's get back," the leader said.

As Troy looked toward the others, he suddenly noticed something which gave him hope. The rope that was used to secure him was wet with rain and failed to hold the knot. With just a little maneuvering, Troy had his hands free. He chose a moment when everyone else's attention was diverted, then spurred the animal he was astride. He pulled it around and started at a full gallop away from the posse. For the first few yards he had the advantage of having the stagecoach between him and the posse, and that masked their fire. By the time the posse galloped around the stage, he had opened up enough distance between them so that only the best marksman could have hit him, and Troy instinctively knew that there was not a crack shot among them.

It was clear to Troy that Alex's horse was the fastest of the lot. The horse ran easily along the winding mountain road. The trail became rocky and rough, necessitating a decreased speed, but that also affected the pursuers.

Finally, the road leveled off, stretching out across open meadow land. There Troy was able to let the horse out to a full gallop. Troy was light and wiry, and the horse was strong and fast. His pursuers were, for the most part, bigger men, thus burdening their horses with additional weight. Troy's advantage told clearly after a few miles, and by the time the open meadow was crossed, and he gained the trees on the other side, he had completely lost the posse.

He dismounted to allow his horse a chance to regain its wind and breathed a sigh of relief. He had made good his escape.

But now he was a wanted man, wanted for killing Alex's father. And the worst blow of all was that Alex believed Troy was the killer.

CHAPTER FOUR

Rice Pendleton had been a very popular man. As stage driver he was also the mailman, so he knew all the citizens of Roseburg and Ashland and nearly everyone in between. Because of that, and since a funeral was a social event as surely as a wedding or a spring dance, there was a great crowd at the graveyard when he was buried.

Reverend E. D. Fisher, who had been preaching in the community for twelve years, had never seen such a crowd, and he bristled with pride and preached his best sermon at the graveside. It was entitled "Jesus, the First Pioneer", and it was particularly appropriate for the pioneers of western Oregon. He thought it went especially well, and was pleased by the number of wet eyes he saw, for a moment forgetting that the tears expressed sorrow over the death of a fine man, and thinking instead that they had been moved by his words.

Alex stood at the graveside for a long time, even after the others had gone, and looked at the pile of dirt that covered her father. She had wept bitter tears of grief for the past four days, but now her eyes were dry, and her sorrow was numbed. There remained only anger at the brutal and senseless murder, and deep inside, Alex vowed to get the man responsible for her father's death.

"Alexandria, dear, we must be going soon if we are to make it to Medford in time for the train." The woman who spoke was in her late thirties, very pretty and perfectly groomed, dressed all in black.

"Very well, Aunt Pricilla," Alex answered.

"Your Uncle Tobias has hired a fast team and a carriage. The roads are quite good, I'm told, so we should make it with little difficulty. I must say, too, that I shall be very glad to quit this place; it is most depressing."

"Funerals always are," Alex said.

"Of course, the funeral is depressing," Pricilla said. "It was sad to have to say a final goodbye to my dear, late sister's husband. But I didn't mean that. I mean this whole place is depressing. The squalid little towns, the dreary mountains, the unending rain. I must admit that I was pleasantly surprised to see that the sun had come out for your father's funeral. Well, thank the Lord for small favors."

"I like it here," Alex said stubbornly,

"I know, dear, you made your point perfectly clear to the judge when he issued the order remanding you to my care until your twenty-first birthday," Pricilla said. "But I know that you'll love Denver even more. We have so much more to offer there. Beginning, I might say, with places in which to buy you some decent clothes. It was most fortunate that Mrs. Tanner was able to make that dress for you in time for the funeral, otherwise you would have had to come in men's pants. It is absolutely scandalous the way your father allowed you to dress."

"It is difficult to drive a stage in a dress," Alex said.

"Yes, to be sure," Pricilla answered. "Oh, here comes Tobias now. If we start right away, we should make the train in plenty of time."

Tobias was a man in his early forties. He was broad across the shoulders and narrow in the waist, and he had big arms and hands, products of his work as a lumberjack when he was young. Tobias had brains as well as brawn, and while the other lumberjacks spent their money on whiskey, Tobias bought timberland and sawmills. By the age of twenty-eight he was a wealthy man. He moved to Denver and managed his business from there, but he was not above going into the woods or even climbing to the top of a Ponderosa pine to top it off if need be. Though welcome because of his wealth in the finest homes in Denver, Tobias Barnett still looked and thought like a lumberjack, much to the chagrin of his wife.

"Alex, I see you stood up to the funeral all right," Tobias said, running one hand through his prematurely silver hair, and holding the reins with the other.

"Of course, she stood up to it," Pricilla said. "What a foolish thing to say."

"Ah, I just don't like funerals," Tobias said. "They are brutal affairs, and I swear if you give me one, I'll come back to haunt you. Climb aboard, ladies, we've got to hightail it on out of here. Alex, honey, would you like to drive?"

"Tobias!" Pricilla exclaimed. "It is unbecoming for her to drive. And I have asked you not to call her Alex."

"But I prefer to be called Alex," Alex said.

"Yeah," Tobias said. "And it might be unbecoming but if we want to make that train, we're better off with the girl drivin'. You know damn well she's a much better driver than I am."

Alex took the reins from Tobias and clucked to the horses. They leaped into their harness and the carriage was off at a fast clip.

The graveyard where Rice was buried had been laid out on the lower slopes of Mount Nebo. High on the mountain, looking down over the scene, a lone rider sat. He leaned forward in his saddle when he saw the girl leave the graveside and watched her climb into the carriage and drive away. The rider was Troy Elliot, and he had come to pay his last respects to the man he was accused of having killed. He had to stay up on the mountain, because he knew that if he showed himself, he might be gunned down before he even had a chance to speak.

As he thought of that possibility, he pulled a paper from his shirt pocket and looked at it. He had pulled it off a tree, just out of town.

WANTED DEAD OR ALIVE!
TROY ELLIOT Reward;
$1500
Contact Any Wells Fargo Agent

There was also a likeness of him, an artist's drawing, but Troy didn't think it was a good enough likeness to give him away to anyone who didn't already know him. That was the trouble, however. Because of his reputation as a gunfighter, Troy was already well known, and there were few towns he could enter without being recognized. With a dead-or-alive warrant out for him, Troy knew that nine out of ten people would shoot first and ask questions later. And for fifteen hundred dollars, even the most cautious person might be tempted to try to bring him in.

Troy had thought about his predicament for the last few days. He considered turning himself in, but he knew that the circumstantial evidence was too strong against him. And with Grayson Thornbury, a respected lawyer, as an eyewitness against him, Troy knew that he wouldn't stand a chance in court.

Grayson Thornbury, Troy knew, wouldn't have lied about seeing Troy kill the others, unless it was Thornbury himself who had done it. And, Troy reasoned, that would make sense out of the rest of it. Why did he not see the robber approach? Because the robber was already on board the stage, that's why. Troy was convinced of that, because there was no other way to explain what had happened.

He was able to piece it together now. Thornbury had simply climbed out of the passenger compartment and up onto the top of the stage. Troy, meanwhile, was studying the terrain, figuring that any danger would come from there and not from within. Thornbury then knocked Troy out from behind, took Troy's gun and shot Pendleton before the older man had time to react. He halted the team, told the others that there had been an accident or something and got them out. Then he quickly shot them, one at a time, as they stood there helpless and unsuspecting.

Troy was convinced that it had happened that way. But how was he to convince anyone else?

Obviously, he could not. He was a wanted man, and he would be shot down before he could even approach anybody. And even if he survived long enough for a trial, who would believe him, a known killer, over Grayson Thornbury, a respected lawyer, a man who was smooth with words? Nobody, that's who.

Troy knew that the part-time jobs he had held in the past would no longer be available. It was too risky to try to work anywhere, because there was always the chance that he would be recognized. That left two choices for him to consider.

The first was to leave the area completely. Just fork his horse and ride away, maybe down to Arizona, or over to the coast to sign on as a seaman. The second choice was to stay around, but that meant living on the dodge, always running from the law and anyone else with greed and an itchy trigger finger. It also meant, in all probability, that he would be forced into a life of crime in order to survive.

Troy abandoned the first idea completely. He had no intention of leaving the area until he had located Grady, the last surviving member of the gang that had killed his family. And now, along with Grady, there was Grayson Thornbury.

That meant Troy would stick around. He made a vow that he would harm no one, unless his own life was threatened. And he would wage a personal war against Wells Fargo, for they were the ones who put the warrant out on him.

It was two days after the funeral before Troy committed his first job. He chose a secluded spot in which to wait for the stage to Wolf Creek. There was cover and conceal-ment beside the road, a clear stream running nearby, and a stretch of road which would see on average only one traveler a day, besides the regular afternoon stage.

There were wildflowers growing in the meadow near Troy's hiding place and to pass the time he gathered bunches of the red, yellow, purple and white blooms. Then, just when he had a full, luxurious bouquet he heard the stage approaching.

Troy climbed to the top of a rock overhang and crouched down out of sight. It was his plan to descend upon the stage by dropping to its roof from the overhang. That way he would be able to get the drop on the driver and guard with less possibility of gunplay. Troy did not want gunplay if it could be avoided.

The stage approached steadily, and he waited until it was right under him. Then he leaped down, landing lightly on his feet just behind the driver's seat. He pulled his pistol and called out to the driver and guard.

"Stop the stage!"

"What the—? Who are you? Where did you come from?" the driver asked, looking around in surprise, for so lightly did Troy land atop the stage that they neither felt nor heard him.

"I know who it is," the guard said. "He used to work for the company. It's Troy Elliot."

"That's right. Hello, Gene, how are you doing?" Troy asked. "Now stop the stage."

"Right away, Mr. Elliot. Just please don't shoot us like you did the others," the driver said, pulling the team to a halt.

When the coach was at a complete standstill, Troy vaulted over the side and pointed his pistol toward the passengers. "You people in there, get out!" he called.

There were two men and one woman inside, and they quickly climbed out as ordered. One of the men started to reach for his inside coat pocket, and Troy cocked his pistol and pointed it toward him.

"I'm just going to give you my money," the man said in a frightened voice.

"You people can keep your money," Troy replied. "I'm only interested in the Wells Fargo money. Driver, open the strongbox and toss me any money you find there."

"I don't have a key."

"Then throw the box down here," Troy ordered. The drive flipped the box over the side, and it landed at Troy's feet. He shot the lock off, and as he started to open the lid, realized that he was still carrying the bouquet of flowers. He smiled, thinking what a ludicrous picture it must make, him standing there with a pistol in one hand and a bouquet of flowers in the other, robbing a stagecoach.

"Here, miss," Troy said, handing the bouquet to the lady. "I think these are very pretty, don't you?"

"Yes," the woman said, flustered by Troy's action. "Yes, they are quite lovely."

"I thought you might enjoy them," Troy said. He dropped to one knee and rifled through the contents of the box until he found a large brown envelope marked Wells Fargo. He opened it, looked inside, and saw a stack of bills. He smiled as he stood up again.

"Well now," he said. "Yes, I think this will do nicely. Would one of you gentlemen be so kind as to hand the box back up to the driver?"

"You're gonna let us take the box back?" the driver asked in surprise.

"Of course, I am. There's no more Wells Fargo money. Besides, there might be a letter from some cowboy's sweetheart in there, and I would hate to cause him to miss it."

Once the strongbox was in place, Troy indicated that the passengers should board the stage again.

"You mean you're just gonna let us go, like that?" one of the men asked.

"Just like that," Troy said.

"Then why didn't you let the others go? Why did you kill all of them?"

Troy sighed. What was the point in telling them that he didn't do it? He knew that they wouldn't believe him, and it wouldn't do him any good if they did believe him. Finally, with a wave of his pistol he ordered them back on.

"And be quick about it," he added. "Or I might change my mind."

The passengers boarded quickly, and the driver, with one last look at Troy, snapped the whip over the head of his team and the stage resumed its journey.

Troy stood rooted to the spot for a while, watching the stage roll off into the distance, followed down the road by a billowing cloud of dust.

Finally, when the stage was out of sight, he allowed himself the luxury of taking the money out of the envelope. There was a small packet of bills, wrapped in a paper band. When Troy counted the money, he found that he had exactly $138.00. Not very much money with which to launch a life of crime. But then, this wasn't a vocation he had chosen willingly, so it really didn't matter. All that mattered was that he had enough for a little food and supplies, and enough to buy a horse so he could return Alex's horse to Oak Grove. After all, he wasn't asking for much. Just enough to keep body and soul together until he located Grady. That was all he wanted. After that, he'd see to Grayson Thornbury.

CHAPTER FIVE

The table in the Barnett dining room was larger than any Alex had ever seen before, larger even than the great common table at Oak Grove way station, and that one could accommodate all the passengers from two stagecoaches, should two arrive at the same time.

Alex wondered when she first saw it why anyone would have a table so large if they had no intention of turning their private dining room into a restaurant. But that question was answered for her the second week she was in residence with her aunt and uncle, when Pricilla gave a party to introduce Alex to all of the "correct people", and to one young man in particular.

All of the "correct people" were there that night. In fact, the guest list read like a Who's Who of Denver society. The most important guests were Mr. and Mrs. Ephraim Kennedy and their twenty-two-year-old son, Denis. The Kennedys were in banking and railroads, and Denis, recently graduated from Harvard University, was ostensibly in business with his father, though in fact and by his own admission he was living off his father's generosity. Denis was handsome, but with a jaded face which rarely showed interest in anything. Until tonight, that is, when Denis displayed a decided interest in Alex.

Mr. and Mrs. Calvin MacDonald were also present at the party, with their eighteen-year-old daughter, Hannah. There were two other girls the same age as Alex; Betsy, the daughter of Mr. and Mrs. Jebidiah Bacon, and Gladys, whose parents were Mr. and Mrs. Godfrey Lohman. All were wealthy, though none were as wealthy as the Kennedys. The MacDonalds, Alex had already decided, were the biggest snobs. There were other guests, but Alex had already forgotten their names.

There were four beautiful silver candelabra on the table, each with eight graceful tapers burning brightly. The soft golden lights of the candles were reflected in the silver, china, and crystal. The meal consisted of marvelous French dishes, served to the diners by a parade of servants who moved in a steady flow from the kitchen to the dining room.

"Mrs. Barnett, this is a perfectly marvelous meal," Ephraim Kennedy said.

Alex had never seen people so elegantly dressed as those here tonight. Despite her initial reluctance to abandon the pants and shirts she loved, she had to admit that it gave her pleasure to be wearing a dress as beautiful as that worn by any of the other women.

"Thank you, Mr. Kennedy, I will tell Monsieur Dubois. I am certain he will be pleased."

"I must say, you had singular good fortune to acquire Monsieur Dubois from the Marshall House. Their dining room has not been the same since he left their employ."

"Mr. Kennedy, I wouldn't think you could even consider patronizing the Marshall House now," Pricilla said in a shocked voice.

"Why?" Mrs. MacDonald asked, her eyes lighting up at the possibility of learning some new gossip.

"Oh, my dear, you mean you haven't heard?" Pricilla answered, her voice registering her displeasure. "They have hired a female piano player to 'entertain' the guests."

"You don't say," the woman answered, reflecting Pricilla's shock.

"But she is quite a good pianist, actually," Denis Kennedy put in. "I think it makes for a rather pleasant evening," he added, looking directly at Alex, almost as if inviting her to go with him.

"Nonsense," Pricilla said, missing Denis's obvious play for Alex. "The place for that kind of thing is in the theatre, for then a person is forewarned, and prepared to be scandalized."

"Oh, I wouldn't go so far as to say that the theatre is scandalous," Ephraim Kennedy protested mildly.

"Now a bawdy house, perhaps," Tobias put in with a chuckle. "I must confess to having heard some really fine piano playing in a few of those establishments in my wild youth."

"Tobias, really!" Pricilla gasped, absolutely shocked and livid that her husband would make such a remark.

While the men laughed, the women stared at their plates in embarrassment—all except Alex, who had trouble stifling her own laughter. Pricilla was so prissy that the remark served her right.

Prissy, Alex thought. Yes, that would be Pricilla's secret name from now on. Aunt Prissy.

"I was just making a small joke, dear," Tobias said easily.

"I must say that the joke was in extremely poor taste," Pricilla said angrily. Then because she realized that to carry her anger any further would have been a social faux pas, Pricilla fixed a smile on her face and looked at the others. "You will have to forgive my husband," she said. "I think sometimes that the rowdiness of those ruffians who work for him is infectious. It is unfortunate that one must come in contact with such people in the pursuit of honest business."

"Yes, my dear, that is certainly true," Mrs. MacDonald said, making a show of agreeing with Pricilla, though actually carrying on the conversation merely to prolong Pricilla's discomfort. "I know I simply cringe when one of our people comes to the house to see Calvin on a business matter," Mrs. MacDonald said the words "our people" possessively, patronizingly. "And I keep Hannah out of sight, for the freight drivers are so uncouth."

"You're hitting the nail on the head on that point, I'd say," Alex pitched in, glad that the conversation had finally reached a subject with which she was familiar. After all, she was certainly more qualified than any of the others present to talk about freight drivers. And how was she going to satisfy her aunt's wish to meet the others on equal terms if she never spoke a word?

"I'm quite sure," Pricilla said, rather stiffly.

"Please, do go on, dear child," Mrs. MacDonald said, delighted at this sudden turn of events. Mrs. MacDonald saw Pricilla cringe at the prospect of this wild young mountain girl making a fool of herself. But, Eliza MacDonald thought, it would certainly serve to show the Kennedys, and Denis in particular, that there was really no choice between the MacDonalds' daughter Hannah and the Barnetts' niece, when it came time to think of a marriage partner, Hannah was obviously the better choice.

"Alexandria, I'm sure no one wishes to hear—"

"Oh, but we do, Mrs. Barnett," Hannah said, suddenly,

along with her mother, seeing the potential of the moment.

"Well," Alex said, pleased that she seemed to be making a hit with her aunt's guests, "I've known quite a few freight drivers. And for the most part they are a bunch of drunks and whoremongers, if you know what I mean. Now the stage drivers, why they aren't like that at all. Oh, they'll turn the air blue with their cursing all right. In fact," she smiled, "I've handled a few teams myself that wouldn't respond to any other kind of command. But the stage drivers are generally sober, honest, family men. I imagine it's because stage drivers have the lives of their passengers to be responsible for, whereas freight drivers haul rope, or feed, or something like that, and they just don't take the same pride in their work."

"Alexandria, please!" Pricilla hissed. Alex noticed the strain in Pricilla's voice and was puzzled by it. What had she done wrong? After all, she had finally joined in the conversation, and she had agreed with the woman who spoke. That was only being polite.

"Tell me, Alexandria," Hannah said, leaning forward and smiling with a secret sense of superiority that Alex didn't perceive. "Can you really drive a stagecoach?"

"I hope to smile I can," Alex answered proudly. "Of course, I've never been an official driver, mind. But I reckon I can handle the ribbons about as well as anyone."

"Ribbons?" Hannah replied, puzzled by the remark. "What are ribbons?"

"Oh, excuse me, I forgot that you wouldn't know what I was talking about," Alex explained. "The ribbons are the reins. There are six of them, of course, for a six-horse hitch."

"Six?" Godfrey Lohman said. "My word, how could one handle six reins at the same time? I must confess that I'm not all that comfortable with two reins. That's why I hire liverymen for my rig. Then I just tell them where I want to go."

The others laughed at Lohman's remark.

"Oh, but it's simple," Alex said. "Well, no, not all that simple really, but I mean once you get the hang of it you can do it." She began gathering up the array of silverware which lay beside her plate. "I was wondering what I could do with all this," she said. "Now it'll come in handy."

Alex began lacing the knives, forks, and spoons through her fingers as if they were the reins of the horses; then she held her hands out, showing them to the others. "Now all you have to do is keep the horses pulling even," she said. "Because if you don't, you are likely to get one that's a bit lazy and he'll slack off and let the others do all the work. You can tell by the pressure on the reins who's doing his job and who isn't, see, like this." She moved her fingers to show that she could control each rein individually.

"Alexandria, please! I have never been so mortified in my life!" Pricilla said. She got up from the table, and left the room, dabbing at the tears in her eyes.

Alex was shocked by her aunt's reaction. What had she done? Why was her aunt so upset? She looked at the others, hoping to gain a clue to the reason for her aunt's strange behavior. Most of the others were staring at their plates, as if embarrassed. She thought, however, that she detected a small smile on Hannah's lips. Why? Because she found the situation amusing? Or because she enjoyed having brought discomfort to Alex? And if she did enjoy Alex's discomfort, why? Alex had never done anything to her.

Tobias cleared his throat. "Mrs. Kennedy, would you lead the ladies into the parlor? I believe Monsieur

Dubois has a dessert for you there. And Ephraim, please take the men into the study for brandy and cigars. I'll join you shortly."

"Of course, Tobias, I'd be glad to," Mrs. Kennedy answered. "Come along, ladies."

The dining room cleared in just a few seconds, except for Tobias who sat at the far end of the table, and Alex, at the opposite end, next to where her aunt had been sitting.

"Mr. Barnett, will you require..." one of the servants inquired, sticking his head through the door. Tobias dismissed him with a wave of the hand, and once again the two were alone. There was a moment of quiet, and tears began sliding down Alex's cheeks.

"Honey, don't worry about it," Tobias said gently.

"But, Uncle, what did I do?" Alex asked, her voice nearly breaking on the last word.

Tobias got up from his chair and walked over to her. He put his hands on her shoulders. "You didn't do anything, dear."

"But I must have. Aunt Prissy was so upset. And Hannah was smiling, as if...as if she enjoyed my discomfort."

"Prissy?" Tobias said, laughing. "You call Pricilla, Prissy?"

Alex smiled through her tears. "I'm sorry, it's just sort of a nickname I made up for her."

Tobias threw his head back and laughed out loud. The laughter seemed to do more than anything to relieve the discomfort Alex felt, and she laughed with him.

"I think that's a marvelous name," he said. "Simply marvelous."

"I'm glad you approve, Uncle Toby," Alex said, using for the first time the nickname she'd given him.

"Approve? Yes, but I'm not sure how Pricil...that is,

Prissy, will take it." he said. "Perhaps we'd better keep it our little secret for the time being. Do that for me, and I'll accept my nickname without fuss," he offered with an easy smile.

"All right," Alex answered. "It's a deal."

"Now, Miss Alex Pendleton," Tobias said, helping Alex from her chair, "dry your eyes and go in for dessert. And do me a favor, will you?"

"What?"

"Just stare Hannah MacDonald down. I'd be willing to bet she's the kind who can't meet a good, honest gaze head on. You try that for me, and she'll be laughing out of the other side of her mouth."

"I'll do that, Uncle Toby," Alex agreed. She started out of the room, then stopped and looked back at her uncle. "Oh, and it's good to see that I have a friend here."

"You've always had me, darlin'," Tobias said easily. "And you'll have me all the way."

CHAPTER SIX

As Tobias had promised, Hannah would not return Alex's honest gaze. But Hannah hid her mouth behind her fan and whispered with Betsy and Gladys, and the three young girls giggled and shared secrets that excluded Alex. Or at least she thought that was what they were doing, and the effect was just as devastating to her, so that after a while she got up to leave the parlor, making the excuse that she didn't feel too well and needed some fresh air.

The Barnett home was a huge, two-storied brick house which sat in the midst of three acres of landscaped lawn. The parlor opened through French doors onto a veranda which completely encircled the house, and once outside, Alex strolled along the flagstone deck until she was behind the house. There she kicked off her shoes and climbed up on the waist-high, wide-topped stone fence that guarded the edge of the porch. She sat there, leaning against one of the many pillars that rose to support the roof, and looked out across the gently sloping lawn and into the clear night sky.

There was a quarter moon that night, so its brightness didn't obscure the stars, and Alex enjoyed their diamond shine, scattered across the sky. They were the same stars she could see from Oak Grove way station, and somehow looking at them made her feel close to home. And to her father, whom she missed terribly.

As she thought of her father her sorrow was replaced by a deep hatred for Troy Elliot, and she remembered her resolve to make him pay for what he had done. She pulled her knees up and when she did so, her dress fell back so that her legs were exposed from her knees down. She wrapped her arms around her legs and rested her chin on her knees. The position was comfortable, and the cool breeze felt good against her legs which were too warm because of the dress and all of the petticoats she was forced to wear. She smiled to herself because she knew the pose was probably unladylike, and Aunt Prissy would have a fit if she saw it.

"It's a beautiful night, isn't it?" a man's voice said.

Alex looked toward the sound and saw Denis Kennedy. He was smoking a cigar, and the ash on the end glowed red as he took a puff.

"Yes, it is," Alex said. She made no effort to cover her legs or change her position. She knew that that was probably the proper thing to do, but she had had just about enough of the proper things for one night. She turned to look at the stars again. "That star is my favorite," she said, pointing to a bright orange light. "It looks like a gold nugget that someone just hung in the sky."

"That's Arcturus," Denis said.

Alex laughed. "You named the star?"

"No, I didn't," Denis said. "The stars were named many years ago."

"Are you serious?" Alex asked. "You mean all those stars have names?"

"I wouldn't think all of them have names," Denis said. "There are too many."

"How many?"

"Oh, about nine thousand can be seen with the naked eye," Denis said. "Though we can't see them all from the northern hemisphere."

"How do you know so much about the stars?"

Denis stepped up to the porch rail beside Alex and ground his cigar out, then flipped it over the edge. He looked at Alex and smiled. "That, my dear, is a result of one of the many wasted classes I took at Harvard. It dealt with the heavens and was called astronomy."

"Oh, I wouldn't think that would be a waste of time," Alex said. She looked back at the stars. "I've always loved the stars. I'd like to know more about them."

"Perhaps you'll allow me to teach you," Denis offered.

"Oh, would you?" Alex asked, her voice bubbling over with enthusiasm.

"It would be my pleasure," Denis said. "In that case the class could well prove to have been a blessing and not quite the waste I thought it was."

"What's that star? The one just above Arcturus?"

"Spica," Denis said. "You are a very beautiful young lady, Alexandria."

"Alex," she said.

"What?"

"I prefer to be called Alex."

Denis laughed.

"What is it? What's so funny?"

"You are quite remarkable; did you know that? You're a breath of fresh air. I tell you that you are a beautiful young lady, and instead of huffing up and acting scandalized as proper young ladies are supposed to, even though they never really are, you just correct me on your name."

"I suppose it's obvious after tonight that I don't know how to act like a proper young lady," Alex said, matter-of-factly.

"Then I hope you never learn."

"But I must learn," Alex said, "if I am to make what Aunt Pricilla calls a favorable impression."

"You've already made a favorable impression on me," Denis said. "But I'm not altogether certain your aunt would approve of that."

"Oh, you are the one she most wants me to impress," Alex said. "You're rich, aren't you?"

Denis laughed again. "You do have a disarming candor which is most refreshing," he said. "Yes, I suppose I am rich. Or rather, my father is, and as I am his only heir, that makes me rich as well. I've done nothing to earn it, though. In polite circles I'm known as a ne'er-do-well. Except in those families who have marriageable daughters, there I'm held up as a sterling example of young manhood. You probably noticed at the dinner table tonight how Mrs. MacDonald tried to make me notice the attributes of her daughter, Hannah."

"So that's why!" Alex said, realizing for the first time why Hannah and her mother had so obviously enjoyed her discomfort.

"Ah, so you see the light now, do you?"

"But surely they see no competition from me!" Alex said honestly. "Hannah is so beautiful, and so...so proper."

"You know, if anyone else had made that statement, I would swear she was fishing for a compliment," Denis said, "but from you, it rings with the truth. I think you honestly don't realize how beautiful you really are."

Alex ran her hand through her raven-black hair, then

looked at Denis with confusion in her amber eyes. "But I'm just a mountain girl," she said. "What do I have to offer?"

Denis turned his head toward her, and his face was bathed silver in the sparse moonlight. The jaded, almost hard face she had seen at the dinner table was now soft and sensitive, as if he were showing her a most intimate part of him which he allowed no one else to see. Something in Alex responded to it, and she moved her face toward his. Their lips met, and she felt a tingling, pleasurable sensation run through her. The kiss deepened, and Denis put his hand behind her head and pulled her to him while he ground his lips against hers, until finally the kiss ended.

"I...I'm sorry," Denis said, after he pulled away.

"Why?"

"Why?" Denis laughed. "Why indeed? I'm not sorry, I rather enjoyed it actually. But one must always apologize after such a thing."

"But I wanted to do it too," Alex said. "Doesn't that count for anything?"

"Oh, you had best be careful, dear girl, for such honesty is not known in polite society, and I fear you might be hurt by it."

"My father used to say that the truth never hurt anyone," Alex said. "And he was a pretty smart man."

"You thought a lot of your father, didn't you?" Denis said.

"Of course, I did," Alex replied. "Doesn't everyone love his father?"

"There are, I suppose, degrees of love."

"Don't you love your father?"

Denis put both hands on the wide stone fence and leaned over it, staring up toward the stars. Finally, with a sigh, he answered.

"I don't know, really. I do respect him, but as I have

been such a disappointment to him, I feel that he doesn't love me. And that makes it very hard to love him."

"A disappointment? How?"

"I told you I was a ne'er-do-well," Denis said. "Oh, I've tried various things—managing banks, working as a railroad administrator, puttering around here and there—but I've shown a talent for none of the things my father has spent a lifetime building."

"How do you occupy your time?"

"It turns out that my one talent lies in gambling," Denis said. Alex noticed that a strange new excitement came into his eyes. "I have fantastic luck with cards. I can almost feel the hands the other players are holding, and odd as it may sound, I can even feel what my next card will be. I've no doubt that I could make it as a gambler if I had to. Of course, such a vocation would be unheard of for one of my station. I must confine myself to friendly matches, or else play under an assumed name in the gaming houses over in Chipville."

"Chipville?" Alex said. "Where's that?"

"It's a collection of gambling houses which have grown up about five miles outside the Denver city limits. They moved out there to avoid the do-gooders who are constantly trying to shut them down in the city. People like my mother and your Aunt Pricilla."

"What's it like in Chipville?"

"Like? Oh, there's an excitement that you can feel the moment you step inside one of the establishments," Denis said. "Poker, faro, roulette. And," he laughed, "even the piano playing that upset your aunt. Plus, dancing girls. It's a fine place all right."

"Do you go often?"

Denis rubbed his chin and smiled a conspiratorial smile

at Alex. "A bit more often than I should, I'm afraid. One of these days someone there is going to recognize me, and when they do, there'll be hell to pay."

"Why? You're a grown man, aren't you?"

Denis laughed again. "Yes, I am," he said. "But if my father chose to be obstinate, he could change his will to ensure that I would never get my inheritance except in small, doled-out amounts. No, it would be best for me to present at least the façade of respect for Father's ideas, if not the substance."

"When are you going to go again?" Alex asked.

"I don't know, really, I hadn't thought about it," Denis said. "If I didn't know better, I'd say you wanted to go."

"Oh, yes," Alex said. "Please, Denis, would you take me?"

"Hold on, here," Denis chuckled. "I've got enough trouble protecting my own identity. If I took you, there'd be twice the chance that we'd be recognized. Besides, there's always the possibility that I could convince Father of my genuine repentance if I went alone and was found out. But with you? No, I'm afraid that would generate a scandal that neither you nor I would be able to live down."

"Oh, please, Denis. You've got to take me."

Denis ran his hand through his hair in exasperation.

"Why? Why would you want to go?"

"You were at my aunt's dinner tonight," Alex said. "You saw how well I fit in with Aunt Pricilla's friends. There has to be something better than this. Maybe your gaming houses are."

"I don't know. I'd have to be responsible for you."

"I'd behave just as you wanted me to," Alex promised. "There won't be any trouble. You'll see."

"All right," Denis said. "I'll do it."

"When?"

"When? Well, I don't know. We'll have to work something out."

"There's an art exhibition next Monday night," Alex said excitedly. "It's in the city library, and Aunt Pricilla has suggested several times that I should attend it. We can say you are taking me to see it."

"I don't know. Your aunt may insist upon a chaperone."

"She may," Alex said, "but she also wants me to make a good impression on you. If I tell her you won't hear of a chaperone, she'll give in."

Again, Denis laughed. "Very well, Miss Pendleton," he said, "I shall call on your aunt and uncle tomorrow afternoon, at which time I shall request the pleasure of your company for the art exhibit next Monday."

"Oh, thank you, thank you!" Alex bubbled. "You won't be sorry, Denis, I won't be any trouble at all, I promise you."

CHAPTER SEVEN

Troy walked over to the rock overhang and looked down into the valley far below. There, just coming off the valley floor and starting up the winding mountain road, was the stage. From this distance it was so tiny that it looked like a toy stage and team he had once seen in a store window.

Troy was waiting for the stage at the turn-out just below the crest. It would be a long, exhausting climb for the team and Troy knew that the driver would halt the horses at the turn-out to let the animals rest, to check the brakes before the descent down the other side, and to allow the passengers time to "stretch their legs", a gentle euphemism for walking into the woods to relieve themselves.

It was because they would be stopping that Troy chose this place to wait. It made robbing the stage much easier. That way there would be little chance for the necessity of gunplay, and less chance of anyone getting hurt. And, so far, Troy had harmed no one.

Troy knew that he had at least an hour to wait for the stage so he took some jerky from his saddlebag, unhooked the canteen, and walked over to sit against a tree, eat his lunch and read the Denver paper he had found that morning. The paper was only a week old, and he read it with great interest.

There was a story about President Garfield, who had been in office less than two months and was already embroiled in a bitter battle with Congress over the appointment of Blaine as Secretary of State. Another article discussed the decline of illiteracy. The paper boasted that in 1880 only seventeen percent of the nation was illiterate.

Then Troy saw a story which both surprised and amused him.

> **An interesting experience while riding**
> **as a stage passenger and being held up**
> **at gun-point by the robber, Troy Elliot,**
> **now known as Beau Bandito**

Beau Bandito? Who could ever dream up such a name, Troy thought as he began to read?

> *He came upon us with both guns blaz-*
> *ing, and the reins of the horse held in his*
> *teeth. "Stand and deliver!" he shouted, in a*
> *voice that was both heroic and frightening.*

Troy had to laugh at that. How could he even talk with the reins in his teeth, much less sound off in a voice that was both heroic and frightening? And he wondered if any robber had ever said, "Stand and deliver."

> *"It is Beau Bandito!" the driver shouted*
> *to us in the passenger compartment. His*
> *voice was laced with fear and respect, for*
> *Beau Bandito, whose real name is Troy*
> *Elliot, is known throughout the West as*
> *the deadliest shot alive. It has been reliably*
> *reported that Troy Elliot can shoot the leg*
> *off a fly at fifty paces.*

The coach was stopped, and the passengers were asked to disembark. I must confess to doing so with the greatest trepidation, though the ladies of the stage were strangely devoid of fear. Rather, they seemed taken by the handsome young man who sat astride the horse, holding the brace of pistols leveled at us, looking at us with eyes keen and calculating. He was wearing a hat with a sweeping feather, and he smiled at the ladies, setting their hearts aflutter.

"Ladies, I beg you forgive this intrusion," the bandit said, "but I intend to relieve Wells Fargo of its money, and as it is being transported on this vehicle, there was no other way than to stop the stage. You will forgive me, I trust."

With that statement, the bandit produced small gifts for the ladies: a cameo brooch for the oldest, a golden locket for the youngest, and earrings for a beautiful young lady of eighteen or so. Beau Bandito placed the earrings on the lady himself, planting a kiss upon her lips as he did so. The others gasped in surprise, and the lady in question blushed a brilliant shade of red, but said nothing. Troy Elliot laughed, then took the money from the messenger guard, climbed back onto his horse, and firing both guns into the air, rode away, shouting at the top of his voice, "Beau Bandito strikes again!"

Troy laughed out loud and wondered how anyone could write such a thing. He had never heard the term Beau Bandito, much less used it. And as for kissing one of the lady passengers...well, he had seen a few he would enjoy kissing, true enough.

There was, however, an element of truth to the article. Troy did give trinkets to the ladies, bits of glitter he'd buy from itinerant drummers. It had started as an accident, when he had given the bouquet of flowers to a young woman during his first robbery. Afterwards he reasoned that if he could keep the ladies from being too frightened, the men would be less likely to do anything rash. And the less likely they were to try something, the fewer chances of anyone getting hurt.

Troy read a while longer, then walked over to check on the approach of the stage. He guessed that it would reach its stop within another ten minutes or so.

Troy heard the pop of the driver's whip and realized with a start that the stage was nearly upon him. He walked over to his horse, patted it gently, then swung into the saddle. "Are you ready, boy?" he asked. "Here it comes."

Troy rode into the trees and waited there for the stage to reach the turn-out. It arrived a moment later, the horses snorting tiredly, straining into the harness.

"Whoa, hold it up there, team," the driver shouted, pulling on the reins. The stage rumbled to a stop. "Folks," the driver called down. "We gotta let these here animals get their wind back before we start down the other side. They's a real purty view from up here, so why don't you take a break and stretch your legs a mite?"

Four people left the stage, two men and two women. One man was obviously a farmer, and as far as Troy could tell unarmed. The other was small and mousey-looking, the type usually found keeping books in dry goods stores. Of the two women, one was an attractive female of forty or so, and the other a beautiful young girl of around eighteen. Troy imagined that the older woman was the younger one's mother, as they looked somewhat alike, and stayed together as they moved away from the stage. There was obviously no danger from any of the passengers.

Troy turned his attention to the driver and guard. The driver was not wearing a sidearm, and was near the lead horses, adjusting a loose harness. The shotgun guard had leaned his gun against the front wheel and took several steps away from it to stretch, to start the circulation back into his legs. The passengers returned to the stage, and Troy thought this would be the perfect opportunity for him to make his presence known.

"Hello, Otis, hello, Fuzzy," Troy said to the driver and messenger, both of whom he recognized from his own days of working for Welles Fargo.

"Elliot," the driver responded.

"Good afternoon, ladies and gentlemen," he said, riding into the clearing. He tipped his hat, but as yet, showed no weapon.

"Oh, my God, he's gonna kill us all!" the meek- looking man said.

"I've no intention of killing anyone," Troy said, "if you follow my instructions."

"What do you want?" the older woman asked. Troy recalled the line in the article, the line he was supposed to have spoken, and he smiled. "Ladies, I beg you to forgive this intrusion, but I intend to relieve Wells Fargo of their money."

"We ain't carryin' much money," the driver said. "Probably no more'n fifty dollars."

"I'm not greedy, Otis, I'll just take what you have," Troy said, still smiling. "Would you get the money for me?"

"I've got some money," the store clerk said, shaking in fear. "I'll give it to you if you spare us."

"Keep your money," Troy said. "I told you, I don't want to hurt any of you."

The driver climbed onto the coach and reached under the seat. He hesitated for a moment, then looked at Troy. A sixth sense, sometimes developed by creatures on the run, told Troy that the driver was thinking of reaching for a gun.

"Don't try it, Otis," Troy said coolly. "You may have less than a second to live."

The driver picked up the pouch and held it and his hands in the air.

"That's better," Troy said. "Now take the money out and hand it to the pretty young lady there."

The driver removed an envelope, and the girl walked over to receive it. While she was doing that, Troy spoke to the shotgun guard. "Fuzzy, would you be so kind as to break open that scatter gun and throw the shells on the ground?"

The guard did as he was told. Troy reached into his saddlebag and took out a pearl pin and a golden locket. He swung down out of the saddle and walked over to the older lady.

"Ma'am," he said politely. "The pearl in this pin brings out the beauty of your eyes. I hope you'll wear it and think of me." He pinned the pearl onto the lady's bodice, and she blinked her eyes and smiled in embarrassment and pleasure.

"And you, Miss," he said, looking toward the younger woman who still held the envelope in her hand, "would you please bring the money to me?" The girl did as instructed. Troy slid the envelope into his pocket, then held up a golden locket, and hooked it around her neck. Again, inspired by the newspaper article, he leaned toward her and kissed her, very lightly, on the lips. He was smiling as he pulled away from her, while she remained immobilized by pleasurable shock.

"Thank you, ladies and gentlemen, for your courtesy." Troy climbed back onto his horse and tipped his hat. "Oh, there's a paper under the tree over there, not more'n a week old. You might enjoy reading it. Goodbye, now." He turned and started away at a gallop. Then, with laughter bubbling out of him, he shouted into the wind, "Beau Bandito strikes again!"

CHAPTER EIGHT

As he had promised, Denis took Alex to one of the gaming houses Monday night. Alex had never seen anything like the Silver Nugget. It was many times larger than the hotel ballroom in Medford, and much more beautiful. She counted at least ten huge crystal chandeliers that, along with the clusters of lanterns on the walls, provided a brightly lit interior. There were tables covered in green felt around which men and women sat playing cards, long tables where they cast dice, and her favorite, the roulette table where a wheel was spun with dizzying speed and the object of the game was to guess on which number the little ball would end up when the wheel stopped. She also saw balconies, spaced at intervals along the walls, where guards armed with shotguns kept watchful eyes on the players.

"What do you think of it so far?" Denis asked, after he had shown her through the place.

"It seems terribly exciting," Alex said. "I can see why—oh, my goodness!" she suddenly said, putting her hand to her mouth.

"What is it?"

"That girl, Denny," Alex said, using the nickname she had given him. "What has happened to the front of her skirt? Someone should tell her. Oh, the poor thing will be so embarrassed." Alex pointed to a beautiful young woman who was carrying a tray of drinks. The front of her skirt was gathered up above her knees, and the red garters on her legs were clearly visible.

"It's supposed to be that way," Denis said. "Don't worry about it."

"Supposed to be that way? Whatever for?"

"She works here. That's part of her costume. Wait until you see the dancing girls, if you think this is something."

"Oh, yes, I'm looking forward to that. I've never seen dancing girls, but I have heard about them."

"You are about to see them," Denis said, "for I notice that the stage is being prepared. Would you like to take a table and have a drink while we watch?"

"A drink? You mean whiskey?"

"Sure, if that's what you want."

"I don't know," Alex said. "I've never tasted whiskey before."

"Why don't you let me order for you?" Denis offered. "I'll pick out something you might like." Denis spoke to one of the girls wearing a cut-away dress, then escorted Alex to a table near the stage. A moment later the drinks came, and Alex saw that hers had a slice of orange and a cherry in it.

"What is this?" she asked. "I've never seen fruit in a drink before."

"It's a house special," Denis said. "Made especially for ladies. I think you'll like it."

"Mmmmm," Alex said, after taking a sip. "You're right. It tastes better than lemonade."

"But it isn't lemonade," Denis cautioned. "So be careful."

Three men came to sit at the table next to theirs, and Alex noticed that they looked her over pretty thoroughly. Finally, one of them leaned forward and, tweaking his mustache, spoke with Denis.

"Tell me, sir, where did you find such a beautiful young lady?"

"She's a...uh...friend," Denis said. "An old family friend."

"Perhaps you'll be so kind as to introduce us to your... family friend," the man said.

"Very well," Denis said. "Her name is Alex. Alex, these three men..."

"Wouldn't gentlemen be more appropriate?" one of the men interrupted.

"These three men," Denis said with emphasis, "are Jack and Nate Curtis, and Wayne Oliver."

"Perhaps you would like to join us?" Jack invited. Jack had been their spokesman. He was around twenty-five with a handlebar mustache and black, slicked-back hair. Nate, his brother, was a younger, smaller copy of Jack, while Wayne had red hair and a pale, rather unimpressive countenance.

"Thank you, no, we wouldn't care to join you just now," Denis said.

"Perhaps just the lady?" Jack asked.

"Certainly not!" Alex snapped. "And I consider it rude of you, sir, even to suggest such a thing."

"Oh ho," Jack said to his partners. "The lady's got spirit. How did she meet up with someone as gutless as Kennedy?"

"Mr. Curtis," Denis hissed. "You are forgetting your end of the bargain, sir!"

"Oh, oh, yes," Jack said. "Shhhh," he whispered to the

others, placing his finger across his lips. "We mustn't give away the secret now, must we? After all, we wouldn't want to kill the goose that lays the golden eggs." He and the others laughed uproariously.

"Denis," Alex said a moment later, after the three men had become engaged in their own conversation. "They know who you are, don't they?"

"Yes," Denis said.

"What did he mean about killing the goose that lays the golden eggs?"

"Ah, he was just talking. He didn't mean anything."

"No, that's not right," Alex said. "They're getting money from you, aren't they? They are getting money to keep your secret."

Denis sighed, and ran his hands through his hair. "Yes," he said. "Yes, they are."

"Why, that's awful! Why are you paying them?"

"You know why. If my father ever gets word of this, I'll be cut off without a cent."

"Then you should just give those men a good thrashing," Alex said.

"Perhaps that's the way your mountain men would handle such a thing," Denis said. "But we do it a bit differently here."

Alex noticed for the first time that Denis was afraid of the three men. She felt sorry for him, and she relaxed the tone of her voice and put her hand comfortingly on his. "Maybe you're right," she said softly. "After all, you have much more experience in handling these matters than I."

A man came onto the stage carrying a megaphone, and he pointed it toward the audience which had now gathered around the tables near the stage.

"Ladies and gentleman," the man said, his voice magnified but distorted by the megaphone. "The Silver Nugget proudly presents the Gilded Lilies of the West."

The music began and a line of girls danced onto the stage. Alex gasped. She had no idea that a woman, any woman, would appear in public dressed as these girls were. They wore what appeared to be brightly colored corsets and nothing else. Their legs were bare from their thighs down, as were their shoulders and arms. The men in the audience whistled and applauded the dancers, who in response smiled and blew kisses back to the men. Alex was spellbound by the entire performance. When it finally ended, Denis spoke to her. "Well, what did you think of it?"

"I've never seen anything like it before," Alex said. "It was...well, exciting, I mean to hear the people in the audience whistle and carry on so. But I don't imagine I could ever do anything like that."

"You mean dance?"

"Yes."

"No, I don't suppose you could. It takes a very special sort of person. It's too bad though, because you are a beautiful girl, and you would be particularly appealing dressed as they were."

"You mean showing off my legs and arms like that? Never. I may not be proper in the sense that Aunt Pricilla wants me to be, but I know that showing that much of your body is wrong."

"Alex, don't abandon your honesty now. It's that refreshing streak of truth in you that I find most appealing."

"I am being honest, Denny. I don't believe I could expose my limbs like that."

"Well, maybe not," Denis said. "Perhaps that manmade

affront to nature has even reached the mountains. Some-day, perhaps a hundred years from now these barriers will all be taken down, and men and women will be as free as the other creatures of nature."

"What are you talking about?"

"I'm talking about this infernal code of modesty about the human body," Denis said. "Of all the creatures in na-ture, only the human being feels shame at nudity."

"And you think one day that will all change?" Alex asked, shocked at the very idea.

"I think clothes will eventually become items which enhance the human body, rather than hide it," Denis said.

"Enhance?"

"Show off," Denis explained. "Show off the parts of the body that we now hide. I only regret," he added with a wistful smile, "that I shall not live long enough to see that day."

Alex suddenly had a mental image of a dress with two round holes through which the breasts could protrude. It was a perfectly ludicrous image, and she laughed aloud at the idea.

At first Denis was surprised by her laugh, then he joined her. Finally, when their laughter had subsided, he invited her to watch him play cards.

They walked over to one of the felt-covered tables, behind which sat a dealer counting the chips out for one of the players. Denis explained quietly to Alex that at the tables he was known by the name of Keller. The chips were red, white and blue, and their stacks caught the artificial light vividly, contrasting sharply with the light-absorbing green felt. The dealer looked up as Denis approached the table.

"Mr. Keller, good evening, sir," the dealer greeted him.

"Will you be joining us?"

"Yes," Denis said. He gave the dealer some money, and the man pushed several stacks of the chips over to him.

"Gentlemen, a new deck," the dealer said, opening a new box of cards. He spread them out on the table in front of the players, then flipped them over expertly. Alex had never seen anyone who was as smooth with cards, and she was impressed.

Finally, the game began. The dealer shuffled the cards and the stiff new pasteboards clicked sharply. His hands moved swiftly, folding the cards in and out until the law of random numbers became the law of the table. He shoved the deck over toward Denis, and Denis cut them, then pushed them back.

"Five card stud," the dealer announced.

Denis won one hundred dollars in the first hand, and a couple of hands later was ahead by five hundred dollars. At that point Jack Curtis joined the game.

"Well," Jack said. "I see Mr. Keller is having a run of good luck."

"He seems to be, yes, sir," the dealer said easily.

"I've had some luck of my own. I wonder who is the luckiest. Perhaps we could find out, with a little show-down?" Jack suggested.

"That would deny the other players an opportunity at the game," Denis said.

Jack looked at the table. There were three other players. "Suppose we take thirty percent from the winning hand, to be divided equally among you three?" Jack said. "What would you say to that?"

"I'd say I'm going to watch a game of showdown," one of the men laughed.

"Me too," one of the others agreed, and the third quickly assented, so that the decision was now up to Denis.

"Very well," Denis said. "You're on."

"How about one thousand dollars on a hand of show-down?" Jack challenged.

"One thousand dollars on one hand?" one of the three around the table said loudly, mentally computing his share of the winner's pot.

"What's that?" someone from one of the other tables asked. "One thousand dollars on one hand?" The news quickly spread from table to table and as each game ended, the other players gathered around the table to watch the card game between the man they knew as Mr. Keller, and Jack Curtis.

The chips were shoved into the center of the table and the cards were dealt. When the hand was finished, Denis won it with a pair of fours.

"A pair of fours," Jack sneered. "It wouldn't have taken much to beat that hand."

"But it was enough to beat yours," Denis reminded him.

"Another thousand," Jack said, sliding the bet forward.

"It's your money," Denis replied easily, pushing his own chips to the middle of the table.

That hand Denis won with a pair of tens.

"Well, you son of a bitch," Jack swore in frustration as Denis raked in the money.

"He may be a son of a bitch," someone from the crowd said, "but he's a card playing son of a bitch. You'd better quit, Jack, while you've still got a shirt on your back."

"And your pants," another shouted, and the crowd roared with laughter.

Jack knew that they were laughing at him, and the thought made him angrier. Finally, he proposed a game of five card showdown for twenty-five hundred dollars, all the money he had left. He slid the money toward the center of the table and stared at Denis. "You can't win three in a row," he said.

Denis matched the money without a word.

"Well, I didn't think you'd have guts enough to do it," Jack snarled.

Denis smiled. "It doesn't take guts, Jack, to play with your money," he said.

Again, the crowd roared with laughter, and Jack's anger grew more intense. "Get on with it!" he said to the dealer.

The dealer dealt out five cards to each of them. There would be no drawing, no opportunity to improve upon the hand drawn.

Jack turned over his cards. He had two pair, Aces and Jacks.

"Ha! I've got you!"

Jack reached for the money.

"Not quite," Denis said, turning over three tens.

Jack stared at the cards for a moment, then his eyes blinked rapidly, as if he didn't believe what he was seeing. Suddenly he let out a yell and jumped up.

"He's going for a gun!" someone shouted, as the watchers started to scramble away from the table. Then the roar of a shotgun exploded from above and behind Alex.

Jack pitched back, overturning a chair, and sprawled on the floor, his chest turning into an oozy mass of blood. Black gun smoke drifted across the room, and the air hung heavy with its unique smell. The house guard who had done the shooting stood in his balcony vantage point from which he overlooked the game and pulled the empty casings from the still smoking chambers of his double-barrel ten-gauge shotgun.

"Are you all right, Mr. Keller?" he called.

"I'm all right," Denis answered. He clutched his hands together to keep them from shaking, and to Alex it looked as if he was about to faint.

"You aren't armed, are you?" the guard asked.

"No, I'm not," Denis replied.

"This man was." One of the men who had been watching the game now bent over Jack's body. He pulled out a short-barreled pistol. "I reckon you saved Mr. Keller's life," he called up to the guard.

Denis closed his eyes and sat perfectly still as they carried Jack's body out of the room. Most of the curious left with the body, and a moment later there was no one left except Denis, Alex and the dealer.

"Denis, we'd better leave," Alex said anxiously.

"What? Oh, yes, I guess so," Denis answered vacantly. But he made no attempt to move.

"Denny, please," Alex said again. "We'd better go."

"The young lady is quite right, Mr. Kennedy," the dealer said quietly. "It wouldn't do for you to be here when the police start asking questions."

"What? You know my name?" Denis asked.

"Of course, sir. Everyone does. But we have respected your wish for privacy. However, if the police come and start asking questions, I'm afraid..." He left the statement unfinished.

"Yes, yes, you're right," Denis said. He stood up, though not without some effort.

"Here is the cash for your chips, sir," the dealer said.

"Oh, you'd better hold out the thirty percent for the..."

"I did, sir," the dealer interrupted him. "You'd best hurry. You can use the back exit."

"All right, thank you," Denis said, putting the money in his pocket. He took Alex by the arm. "Come on."

Alex looked toward the front of the large room, where the staff gathered around Jack's body. "It served him right," she said.

"What?"

"That Jack. He has been cheating you all this time. He's been telling you he would keep your secret, and he took money from you, when all along everyone knew who you were anyway."

"Yes," Denis said. "Yes, I suppose you're right." He put his hand on his forehead. "Let's go, quickly. I'm afraid I'm going to be ill."

CHAPTER NINE

They left through the back door of the Silver Nugget and the cool night air somewhat revived Denis, though another wave of nausea overcame him just before they claimed their buggy, and he had to excuse himself and move quickly into the bushes. He returned a moment later, looking somewhat sheepish, ashen-faced, and dabbing at his lips with a handkerchief.

"Denny, would you like me to drive us home?" Alex asked.

"No," Denis said weakly. He folded the handkerchief and put it away gingerly. "I really should drive."

"But it would be absolutely no trouble for me to drive. And you don't look as if you are up to it."

Denis managed a small smile. "No doubt you could handle the team much better than I could, even if I felt well. But I think that driving will help me shake the nausea and dizziness."

"Was this the first time you've ever seen anyone shot?"

"Yes."

"Then you have absolutely nothing to be ashamed of."

"You took it much better than I did. Have you ever seen

anything like this before?" Denis asked.

"No," Alex said. "But my own father was murdered by a gunman."

Denis put his hand tenderly on Alex's shoulder. "Of course, I had forgotten that for a moment. In a way, this must have been worse for you than it was for me. Oh, Alex, can you ever forgive me for bringing you to such a place? It must have awakened memories which are best left forgotten."

"No, I never want to forget," Alex said. "I want to remember the man who killed my father, so that someday I will be able to stand in the crowd and watch him hang."

The intensity of Alex's remark left Denis speechless for a moment, and when he finally recovered, he moved her gently toward the buggy. "Come on," he said. "We must leave before the law gets here."

As Denis started the team down the back road, the effort to drive did help him to overcome his nausea, just as he hoped it would, and within a few moments, he was feeling much better.

"I see what you mean about your talent with cards," Alex said, hoping to engage him in a conversation which would take his mind off what had just happened. "You were really good. How did you develop such a skill?"

"I can't explain it," Denis said, warming to the subject. "But it's almost as if a mysterious heat comes off the cards when I'm near them. I know which cards are best. I tell you if I were to go broke tomorrow, I wouldn't starve."

"Then why do you worry so about your father cutting off your inheritance?" Alex asked.

Denis laughed. "I don't know. I guess it's just the natural urge to want a great sum of money. Especially if it is yours."

"But it's your father's money, isn't it? Not yours."

"You're right there," Denis agreed. "I've always had a feeling of guilt over knowing that I will be wealthy someday as the result of my father's toil, and not my own. But the guilt has never been strong enough for me to seriously consider abandoning my inheritance."

"Oh, I don't know about that," Alex said.

"What do you mean?"

"Maybe that's why you do the things you do. Maybe you don't have the strength to come right out and abandon your inheritance, but you secretly want your father to take it away from you."

Denis laughed. "It is an interesting thought. Do you know what you are doing now? You are delving into my psyche."

"Into your what?"

"Into my mind, trying to explain why I do certain things. That's called psychology, from the Greek words psyche which means mind, and logos which means the study of."

Now it was Alex's turn to laugh. "Is that something else you learned at Harvard?"

"Yes. It was quite interesting, really. A man named Wilhelm Wundt has created a whole new field with his work in psychology. It is a science now, just as astronomy is a science."

"You mean there are people who do nothing except try to figure out what other people are thinking about?" Alex asked.

"What they are thinking and why," Denis answered.

"What a foolish waste of time."

"On the contrary. The subject is quite fascinating, actually. And even you engage in it, though without giving it a name."

"Maybe I should go to Harvard and study this," Alex laughed.

"Oh, wouldn't I like to see that though?" Denis said. "Unfortunately, women aren't allowed at Harvard."

"Why?" Alex asked, bristling quickly. "Don't they think women are smart enough?"

"There are schools of thought on that subject, too," Denis said. "The male brain is somewhat larger than the female brain; therefore, most scholars believe the male is smarter than the female."

"And you?" Alex challenged. "What do you believe?"

"No, my dear, you aren't going to get me embroiled in this discussion. I was merely giving you the benefit of my studies, not my opinion."

"But I would like to know your opinion," Alex insisted, refusing to relinquish the subject.

"Meeting someone like you, a woman with a keen, analytical, though unschooled mind, makes me ready to develop a theory which is contrary to prevailing thought and say that among women, as among men, the degree of intelligence is based upon individual development, and not predetermined by sex."

Alex smiled. "I think you are saying you don't really believe that men are smarter than women."

"Not as a group, no, I don't think men are smarter than women," Denis said. "Though Alex, if you ever bring this subject up at one of your aunt's social functions, I will swear that this conversation never took place."

"Aha," Alex said. "I thought so. It turns out that you're really no diff—"

Bang!

Alex's sentence was interrupted by a gunshot, and the

sudden appearance of two horsemen in front of the buggy. The horses reared at the loud noise, and it was all Denis could do to bring the animals under control.

"You idiots, what are you trying to do, kill us?" Denis shouted angrily as he fought to quiet the team.

"Now that might not be such a bad idea, since you caused my brother to be killed."

"Curtis!" Denis cried, now recognizing the two riders. One was Nate Curtis, and the other was Wayne Oliver. "

"You know very well that Denis had nothing to do with your brother's death," Alex said. "He was killed by the guard, and he had it coming to him. He was going for a gun to shoot Denis."

"That was his mistake," Nate said. "He thought Kennedy was enough of a man to fight his own battles, rather than have someone else do it for him. I won't make that same mistake."

"Don't be absurd," Denis said. "I couldn't very well fight your brother; I wasn't even armed."

"Well, we're going to fix that right now," Curtis said. "Wayne, do you still have that little pepperbox stuck up your sleeve?"

"Yeah, I got it, Nate. But you know that's just for emergencies."

"Well, this is an emergency. Take it out and give it to Kennedy. I want him armed when I kill him."

"What?" Denis asked, gasping in quick fear. "What are you talking about?"

"I'm going to kill you," Nate Curtis said as easily as if he had just announced that he was going to brush the dust off someone's coat. "But you will be armed, so it will be a fair fight."

"Armed, with a pepperbox?" Alex said. "That's a

woman's firearm."

"Well, then it should be appropriate, don't you think?" Nate asked with a laugh. Then the smile left his face. "Give him the gun, Wayne."

For just a moment Nate took his eyes off the two and looked over toward Wayne, and Alex, who had been waiting for her chance, took that opportunity to make her move. She grabbed the buggy whip and used it to knock the gun cleanly out of Nate Curtis's hand. The buggy whip was not much more than a riding quirt, so she had very little mechanical advantage with it. How she wished for one of the bullwhips that she used to drive the stage! With it she could have jerked Nate Curtis out of the saddle. As it was, the gun was all she could manage.

"What the hell?" Nate shouted, watching his gun flying toward the side of the road.

Alex grabbed the reins and snapped against the back of the team. "Heah!" she shouted.

The team bolted forward as if fired from a cannon, and by the time Nate Curtis retrieved his pistol, he knew that the buggy had too great a lead for them to overcome.

The escape having been successful, by the time they reached Denver, Denis was driving again. He turned off the road and pulled the buggy up the great, curving, white chipped gravel driveway that described a large arch from the road to the front of the Barnett home. A few seconds later, they stopped by the front porch, and her uncle's groom held the team while another helped Alex step down from the buggy. She looked up at Denis, who still held the reins.

"Denis, won't you come in for a while?"

"No, thank you," Denis said. "I think I'd better be

getting back."

"Nonsense," Alex said in a tone that indicated that she felt strongly that he should come in. "You come in and visit with my aunt and uncle for a short time."

"Very well," Denis said. "If you're certain I won't be intruding."

As the two walked up the steps and across the porch, Denis spoke to her softly: "I don't think this is such a good idea. What if they ask me questions I can't handle?"

"If you can't handle them, I'll answer them," Alex said, realizing at that moment that though Denis was older and better educated, she had become the dominant personality in their relationship.

Her aunt and uncle were waiting in the parlor, and they greeted the young couple as they entered.

"Alexandria dear, did you have a nice time?"

"Yes, a very nice time."

"Denis, would you care for a brandy?" Tobias offered.

"Yes, thank you, that would be very nice," Denis accepted, realizing that he needed a brandy tonight of all nights.

"How was the art exhibit?" Pricilla asked.

"We didn't go to the exhibit," Alex said easily.

"What? Well, I don't understand. I thought that was where you were going."

"We changed our minds," Alex said. "Instead, we went to see a show."

"A show? But Alexandria, that's scandalous. That simply isn't done," she said, her tone of voice clearly showing her shock. "Denis, how could you!"

"It wasn't his fault, Aunt Pricilla," Alex said quickly. "I teased him to do it. I've never seen one, and I so wanted to."

"Well, I had never seen one when I was your age either," Pricilla said, still shocked by the revelation. "And I only see them now if I know they are for charity or some other worthwhile cause."

"Oh, leave them alone, Pricilla," Tobias said gently. "Times have changed. The young people enjoy getting out more now than they did when we were young."

"Still, to go see a show—and unchaperoned. I'm just terribly fearful of what others might say."

"The others be damned!" Tobias said.

"Tobias, please, such language isn't called for, even under these rather trying conditions."

"What did you see?" Tobias asked easily.

"We saw a dance program," Alex said. She looked over to Denis and saw that he was smiling into the brandy snifter, despite himself.

"A dance?" Pricilla said. "Well, thank heaven for small favors at least. A dance is infinitely more to be preferred to a play, or, heaven help us, this new thing called a 'review' that features all sort of vulgar events. But Alexandria, dear, you are still unschooled in the social graces, so please, before you do anything else foolish, at least consult with me."

"Yes, Aunt Pricilla," Alex answered obediently.

"And as for you, young man," Pricilla said, facing Denis.

"Yes, ma'am?"

Pricilla smiled an ingratiating smile. After all, here was the prize catch of Denver, and he seemed to be taken with her niece, regardless of Alexandria's obvious social ineptitude. Perhaps it wouldn't do to let her anger spill over onto him.

"As for you, I am pleased at least, that you were with her. I know that regardless of her unfamiliarity with life, she is safe with you as her guardian."

A sudden cloud descended over Denis's eyes, and he looked away with a feeling of guilt for having exposed her, not only to the gambling, but to a man being shot, then being accosted on the way back home...a situation which would have been much more dire, had Alex not saved the day.

"I, uh, mean merely, that I want to thank you," Pricilla said seeing his reaction, and trying desperately to undo whatever she had done with her remark.

Alex realized immediately what Denis was thinking, and she walked over to him and put her hand possessively on his arm. "Aunt Pricilla, I saw the show only because I was escorted by Denis. I had confidence that with him as my guide, there would be no talk to embarrass you."

"Very well, dear," Pricilla said. "But please, in the future, try to think of all the possible consequences before you embark on any folly."

"I will, Aunt Pricilla, I promise."

CHAPTER TEN

"I'll give you fifteen hundred dollars to kill Troy Elliot."

Grady was talking to Eli Watson, Frank McBean, and Gus Condon.

"Ha, you say you'll be givin' us fifteen hunnert dollars to kill 'im, but it won't be you that's doin' it, Mister, we done seen the dodgers that's out on 'im. There's already a fifteen-hundred-dollar reward for anyone who kills 'im," Watson said.

"I'm sorry if I didn't make myself clear," Grady said. "I meant that I would match the fifteen-hundred-dollar reward, with another fifteen-hundred- dollars. That would be three thousand dollars, or a thousand dollars apiece."

Watson, McBean, and Condon looked at each other.

"A thousand dollars apiece! We'll do it!" Condon said.

"Where's he at?" McBean asked.

"I don't know where he is. Part of collecting the reward is in finding him."

Over the next six weeks, Condon, Watson, and McBean began checking every saloon in every town between Eugene City and Ashland. They had no idea what he looked like, so they started asking, though since they were sure he wouldn't be using his real name, their only chance to find him was to find someone who knew him.

They went into the Columbia Saloon in Medford, and as they had in every saloon they had been in so far, began asking questions.

"How much is it worth to you if I tell you where he is," a rather short man with a gray beard and long gray hair asked.

"A hunnert dollars, if it's really him," Watson said.

"Make it a hunnert 'n' fifty, 'n' I'll tell you where he is."

"That'd be fifty apiece," McBean said to Watson.

"Who are you, 'n' how do you know 'im?"

"My name is Hank Kitchen. I used to work as a hostler at the Rock Point way station. I seen 'im lots o' times when he would come in as a shotgun guard."

"Where is he?"

"I seen 'im in Jacksonville this mornin'. I know he's still there, 'cause he's took a hotel room. He's callin' hisself Cary Stanton."

"All right, we'll go check it out," Watson said.

Kitchen held his hand out. "I'll take my hunnert 'n' fifty dollars now."

"Not yet. You're goin' to have to come to Jacksonville with us, 'n' point 'im out."

"Point 'im out?" Kitchen said in a frightened voice. "Why, if he seen me do that, he'd kill me."

"Not if we kill him first," Watson said with an icy smile. "And that's the only way you're goin' to get you one-hundred and fifty dollars."

The distance between Medford and Jacksonville was only five miles, and the four men covered it within less than half an hour. They tied off their horses in front of the Pioneer Saloon.

"Take a look 'n' see if you see 'im in there," Watson said.

Troy was sitting at a table, nursing a beer and wondering what happened to Alex Pendleton. She had just disappeared on him, but as things had developed, that was probably just as well. She hated him because she thought he killed her father.

He couldn't blame her for feeling that way, if she really did think he had killed her father. Grayson Thornbury is the one who accused him, and Troy was certain that Thornbury was the one who killed Rice Pendleton.

As Troy sat there, deep in contemplation, he saw a man with gray hair and a gray beard peer over the top of the batwing doors. Troy couldn't place him, but he had the feeling that he had seen him before. He didn't have the opportunity to study it though, because the man made one quick glance, then disappeared.

"He's in there, all right," Kitchen said, when he stepped back outside. "He's wearin' 'im a green shirt, 'n' he has his hat a' sittin' on the table. He's back near the piano."

Watson, McBean, and Condon went into the saloon then, and the three of them stepped up to the bar.

Troy saw them come in, and because he was being extra cautious now, he looked at them for a moment. That was when he saw that all three of them were studying him, in the mirror.

Finally, one of them turned around.

"Is your name Troy Elliot?"

The man who questioned him had a handlebar mustache that drooped around his mouth.

Hearing a name that nearly everyone in the saloon

recognized, several turned to look at him.

"Nope, you've got the wrong man," Troy said. "The name is Stanton, not that it's any of your business."

"I think you're lyin' to me. I think you're Troy Elliot, 'n' I'm figurin' on killin' you for the reward. What do you say, Mr. Elliot? Me and you. You want to try it now?" The man who had challenged Troy was Eli Watson, but of course, Troy had no way of knowing that. Watson moved his hand down to hover just over his own gun.

From a nearby table a woman's laughter halted in mid trill and the piano player pulled his hands away from the keyboard so that the last three notes of his melody hung raggedly, discordantly, in the air. All conversation ceased and everyone in the crowded saloon turned to see if the event they had all been speculating on was about to take place.

"Well, mister, if you are challenging me, that wouldn't be a fair draw now, would it?" Troy asked, replying to the man's challenge. "I mean I'm sitting down, and you're standing up. I would be at a disadvantage trying to draw."

Watson flashed an icy smile. "Yeah, well, that's just the way it is. Now I'm tellin' you to go for your gun and I ain't goin' to wait around all day waitin' for you to take me up on it."

Troy made no move toward his own gun, but he did smile at Watson, and his smile was even colder and more frightening than that of the man who was challenging him.

"But you see, the thing is, I don't have to go for my gun," Troy said. "I already have it out. I'm holding a gun under this table right now and it's pointed straight at your gut."

Watson blinked a couple of times, then he laughed nervously. "Who the hell are you trying to kid, Elliot?"

he asked. "You ain't got no gun in your hand." With his left hand, he pointed. "Hell, I can see your gun in your holster, plain as day!"

"Really? Well, I'm not talking about that gun," Troy explained. "What I'm talking about is the holdout gun I keep up my sleeve. It's a Derringer, two barrels, forty-one caliber. I can shoot right through this table and put a hole in your belly big enough to reach into and pull your innards out. I'm sure you know what one just like this gun did to Abraham Lincoln."

"You're bluffin'. You ain't got no holdout gun under there. I know you ain't."

"You might be right," Troy said. "It could be that there's nothing under here. On the other hand, it could be just what I said it was."

"You expect me to believe you?"

"It really doesn't matter whether you believe me or not. Go ahead, try it now and let's get this over with so I can shoot you, then get back to my drinking."

Watson stood his ground for a moment longer, trying to decide whether or not he would call Troy's bluff. His eyes narrowed, a muscle in his cheek twitched, and sweat broke out on his forehead.

"Hell, let's do it," McBean said as he and Condon turned around. "That derringer only has two shots, 'n' there's three of us."

"Watson, ask them which one of them wants to die. You are going to die and one of them will. Ask which one of them is willing to do it."

"Does this son of a bitch have a holdout gun under the table, or doesn't he?" Watson asked.

"I doubt it," McBean said.

"Thank you, Mister, you've just helped me make up

my mind who I'll kill after I kill Watson here," Troy said.

"If we all three draw at the same time, he can't kill all of us," Condon said.

"But, Condon, you dumb son of a bitch, he can kill two of us," Watson said.

"He's right, Condon, I can kill two of you. And you just might be the second one I kill."

"Shit!" Watson shouted. He put his hands out in front of him. "All right, all right, I ain't goin' to go for my gun now, so don't shoot. Don't shoot 'cause if you do, it'll be murder. Come on, let's get out of here."

"Watson?" Troy called out as the three men started to leave.

Watson turned toward Troy.

"Don't make another foolish move like that."

Troy watched until all three of the men had disappeared through the swinging batwing doors. Then he brought his hands up from under the table. They were completely empty. When the others in the saloon saw this, they burst out into loud, raucous laughter. Some applauded.

Smiling to acknowledge their applause, Troy got up from the table and walked over to the bar. He handed the bartender his empty mug, requesting a refill, and as the bartender walked down to the beer barrel to refill the mug, Troy turned toward the door and, calmly, waited.

"You son of a bitch!" Watson shouted, and the three of them, with guns in hand, darted back inside the door. All three of them fired toward the table where Troy had been a moment earlier.

"I'm over here, boys," Troy said calmly, standing at the bar, now holding his pistol in hand.

Then, realizing that Troy had moved, the three men turned toward him for a second shot.

Not one of the three men got a second shot off.

Troy fired three quick shots, so fast that nobody could hear the individual shots, just a sustained roar. All three of Troy's would-be assailants went down.

There were heavy footfalls on the boardwalk as the sheriff came running up to the saloon. Seeing Troy standing over the bodies with a pistol in his hand, he stopped.

"I don't reckon I even need to ask who done this," he said.

"I did it," Troy replied easily.

"Sheriff, this fella had no choice," the bartender said. "All three of 'em come in here at the same time, gunnin' for him."

"Why would they do that?" the sheriff asked.

"They thought I was Troy Elliot. It was a case of mistaken identity," Troy replied.

CHAPTER ELEVEN

"Denis asked me to grant my permission for him to ask you to marry him," Pricilla said. "I told him of course he has my permission," she added with a pleased smile.

"Yes, I know. He's already asked me."

"Oh, how wonderful! We'll have the biggest and most grand wedding Denver has ever seen!"

"I told him no."

"You did what?" Pricilla shouted.

"I turned him down."

"How could you? Don't you realize that is what I have been grooming you for all this time?"

"I don't love him, Aunt Pricilla. I like him, I respect him, I think he is a very fine man. But I don't love him."

"Oh posh. What does love have to do with it?"

Alex turned twenty-one less than two months after she told her Aunt Pricilla that she had no intention of marrying Denis Kennedy. She was now old enough to be on her own, and when she expressed her wish to return to Oregon, her Aunt Pricilla offered no objections.

Neither her aunt nor her uncle came down to the train

station to see her off. Denis, who she still considered her friend, and Hannah MacDonald had come to tell Alex goodbye.

"I wish you were able to stay longer," Denis said. "I'm going to miss you. We're going to miss you," he added.

"I'm going to miss you as well," Alex said. "But I miss Oregon, and I want to go home."

Denis and Hannah stood on the platform as Alex boarded, and remained to wave at her as the train got underway.

Three days after she boarded, Alex left the train at Medford, to take the Wells Fargo stagecoach from Medford to Canyonville. Now, riding the stage from Medford to Canyonville, she was ready to pick up the reins of a new life.

There were three other passengers in the coach. Sitting next to her was a woman, perhaps five years older than she, travelling with her six-year-old son. The woman was pretty and friendly, but quiet, and Alex was grateful for that, as she was not in a talkative mood, but rather reflective on what lay ahead for her.

The boy was very active, as all six-year-old boys are on long trips, and continually changed seats from one side of the coach to the other. Directly across from Alex sat a fat, red-faced man who held a handkerchief with which he constantly wiped at the sweat which dampened his forehead. He wore a suit and vest and carried a watch in his vest pocket secured by a gold chain. He took the watch out several times, opened it, then snapped the case shut, as if calling attention to his fine timepiece.

He had just finished checking the watch for perhaps the fifth time, when he cleared his throat. "We appear to be right on schedule, I see," he said.

No one answered his comment.

"You see the little town ahead of us, lady?" he asked.

His question was directed to Alex, and she had no choice but to answer him. She tried to discourage him by using a one-word answer. "Yes."

"It's called Canyonville," the man, who Alex surmised may have been a salesman, said. "You might not think it, but it's about the widest open, wildest town I've ever seen."

No answer.

"And believe me," the drummer went on, undiscouraged, "I've seen a few wild towns in my days. Fact is, I've tamed a few, back in the days when I was a lawman."

"You were a lawman?" the wide-eyed boy asked.

"That I was, lad," the drummer answered, appreciative that someone, even a child, had shown an interest. "And I know wild towns when I see 'em. Why this town here is so bad that a single lady—you are a single lady, aren't you, ma'am?" he asked Alex, then went on without waiting for an answer. "A single lady can't even go out for dinner unescorted, without runnin' the chance of gettin' molested. That bein' the case, ma'am, I'd be glad to take you to dinner tonight."

"Thank you for your concern, sir," Alex replied coolly, "but I would prefer to dine alone."

"Have it your way," the drummer said, wiping the sweat from his forehead. "Far be it from me to try 'n' influence you in any way. But I was talkin' to Troy about it just the other day. Troy, that is, Troy Elliot, you've heard of him, haven't you, ma'am? He's called Beau Bandito by some."

"Yes, I've heard of Troy Elliot."

"Troy Elliot is one of my best friends. Anyway, he told me that one of these days he wanted me and him to get together and clean out some of the riff-raff in Canyonville that's botherin' the ladies now."

"You said you was a lawman," the boy said. "Why didn't you arrest Troy Elliot when you saw him?"

"Because, I told you, he is my friend. And I'm not a lawman anymore."

"Troy Elliot is the fastest man with a gun that ever lived," the boy suggested knowingly. "That's why you didn't arrest him."

"That's almost the truth, son," the drummer said. He leaned back and hooked his thumbs into his vest "But the fact is, I gave him his first shootin' lesson. I've often wondered since then if I did the right thing, seein' as what Troy has become."

"You mean you taught Troy Elliot how to shoot?" the boy asked excitedly.

"That I did," the drummer said. He glanced toward Alex to see how she took this bit of news but she was once again looking out the window, seemingly paying no attention to the drummer's bragging.

"Boy! If you taught him how to shoot, you must be even faster!"

The drummer chuckled. "I wouldn't say I was faster," he said. "Troy caught on real good. In some ways I'd say he's as good as, or maybe even faster, than me. I'd hate to see what would happen if we ever had to face one another down."

"Oh, wow! Would I like to see that!" the boy exclaimed.

"Richard, that's quite enough now," his mother said, addressing him sharply. "Leave the man alone."

"Oh, Ma, I want to hear all about it," Richard protested.

"It's all right, ma'am," the drummer said, beaming under the boy's admiration. "I don't mind tellin' him the story."

"I'm sure you don't," the boy's mother said.

Alex swallowed a laugh by forcing a cough.

"The truth is, son, before I was a lawman, why I'm 'shamed to say I followed a life of crime. I was a gunfighter, but I give that up. You see, that's no life for a man, and I don't want you studyin' on goin' into it. I'm in an honest line of work now. I sell pots and pans. It's a lot more rewardin' than killin'."

"How many men did you kill?" Richard asked.

"I guess eight or nine," the drummer said. He flipped his jacket back and patted the handle of his gun. "I used to have the handle notched, but that just invited the young gunfighters who were tryin' to make a name for themselves to try me out, so I took that handle off and put a new one on."

"What about Troy Elliot? How many men has he killed?"

"Probably ten or eleven by now," the drummer said. "Though I can tell you that every one of 'em needed killin'. Troy's not the sort to kill for the fun of it."

Alex bit her lip to keep from speaking out at that last statement. It was obvious to her that the drummer was spreading tall tales, and equally as obvious that no one but the boy believed him, so she had no intention of dignifying it by discussing Troy Elliot with him.

"I wish Troy Elliot would hold up this stagecoach," the boy said. "I'd like to see that."

"Oh, I don't think he would do that," the drummer replied. "If he saw me, he'd have to back off."

"Why?" the boy asked.

"Because I'd have to protect this stage, and you and the two ladies. That means Troy Elliot and I would have to go up against each other. It would be friend against friend. And I don't know who would win. No, sir, I don't think there is any danger of Troy Elliot hittin' this stage."

As the drummer spoke the last word a shot rang out and there was a sharp exclamation of pain from the driver. The driver shouted at the team, and the stage came to a halt. "Don't spook the team, mister!" the driver said in a pained voice. "I've got women 'n' kids inside, 'n' I'm hit bad. I couldn't stop a runaway."

"Maybe you people inside better come on out here then," a gruff voice said.

"It's a holdup!" the boy exclaimed excitedly, and he opened the door and jumped out before his mother could grab him.

"Richard, come back here!" she called sharply, following him outside.

Alex and the drummer followed them outside, and Alex saw the bandit. He was wearing a long, flowing cape. His head was covered with a flour sack so that his features weren't visible. Alex looked up at the driver and saw that he was holding his chest. Bright red blood was spilling across his fingers.

"You'd better watch out," Richard told the bandit. "You know who this man is?" He pointed to the drummer.

"Richard, that's quite enough!" his mother said.

"Yes," the drummer hissed to the boy. "Don't say anything else."

"Well now, is everyone out?"

"Yes," Alex said quietly.

"Hey, ain't you the pretty one, though?" the bandit said to Alex.

"Allow me to introduce myself, ladies. I am the Beau Bandito."

"Then you must know who this man is," Richard said again.

"Why do you keep sayin' that, boy? Who the hell is he?"

"He's the man who taught you how to shoot," Richard shouted. The drummer eased his way around behind Alex and the boy's mother.

"Taught me how to shoot, huh?" the bandit said, laughing. He holstered his pistol. "Well, then why don't you get out from behind those women's skirts and see if I learned my lesson well?"

The drummer didn't move.

"Come on," Richard urged. "Show him. You can beat him."

"How about it, teacher?" the bandit taunted, opening and closing his fingers just over the handle of his gun. "You wanna give me a test?"

"No, no!" the drummer shouted, ducking behind the two women. His voice climbed to a falsetto in his fear.

The bandit laughed again, a heavy, mocking laugh. "Don't worry. I'm not gonna kill you. I only kill men. You and the other ladies, I'll give presents to." The bandit reached into his saddlebag and took out three lockets. He tossed them casually toward the group of passengers, then laughed. "Here. Here are three presents for you three ladies."

The lockets lay on the ground.

"Pick 'em up, drummer," the bandit ordered.

The drummer recovered the lockets, gave one each to the two women, and slipped the third into his vest pocket.

"That's better. Now climb up on the driver's seat and get the money pouch and hand it over to me."

The drummer climbed up to get the pouch as directed, then he handed it over to the bandit, and the bandit hooked it on the pommel of his saddle. He slapped his legs against his mount and started off at a gallop. "Beau Bandito strikes again!" he called out.

As soon as the bandit was gone, Alex climbed onto the driver's seat to look at the driver. His face was white, and his lips were purple, and he was gasping for breath.

"I'm hit bad," the driver said. "I dassn't try and drive us into Canyonville. If I pass out, the stage could go over the side. Everyone would be killed," he gasped.

"My God," the drummer said. "What are we goin' to do?"

"We've got to get him inside," Alex said. "Help me get him down."

"But who's going to drive us into town?" the drummer asked again. "We can't stay out here forever."

"I'll drive us into town," Alex said easily.

"What? You are goin' to drive this stage? You heard what the driver said. If we go over the side, we'll all be killed."

"Then I'll try not to go over the side," Alex said. "Now help me get the driver down."

Alex, the boy's mother, and the drummer managed to get the driver down from the seat and lay him across the coach seat.

"Jesse, it's me," Alex said to the driver. "Alex Pendleton."

"Alex?" the driver said, coughing up specks of blood. "I didn't recognize you when you boarded the stage, girl. You've changed."

"I may look different," Alex said, "but I'm as good a driver as I always was. I'll take us into town."

"Watch old Ben," the driver warned. "He tries to have his way, and you've got to hold him back going down the grade here."

"Which one is Ben?"

"He's the lead, off horse," the driver said. He started

coughing again.

Alex looked at the other woman. "Stop the bleeding in his chest," she ordered. "And do what you can to make him comfortable."

"All right," the woman said. "Are you really going to drive this coach?" she asked anxiously.

"I thought I might give it a try," Alex said.

"I'm not so sure it's a good idea," the drummer announced. "Maybe I'd better try."

Alex looked at the driver. "You make the decision, Jesse," she said. "Which one of us would you rather have drive?"

"There's no decision to make," Jesse said. "You drive." He coughed again from the exertion of talking.

"I'm not ridin' with any woman driver," the drummer said.

"Suit yourself," Alex replied as she started up to the driver's seat. "Wait around out here if you want. I'll send someone back for you."

The drummer thought for a second, then crawled inside. "All right," he said. "I'll come along. But only because you may need some help."

"Lord help us, let us hope not," the boy's mother said.

"You didn't even try to draw on him," the boy suddenly accused. He had been staring at the drummer the whole time and was obviously hurt to see his idol's image shatter so abruptly.

"What could I do?" the drummer replied. "He had the drop on me."

"He put his gun away," the boy protested. "He gave you a chance to go for it."

"It's an old trick," the drummer said. "He had someone hidin' in the trees who had the drop on me. The moment I went for my gun, his confederate would have shot me down."

"I didn't see anyone in the trees," the boy challenged.

"That doesn't mean a thing," the drummer said. "I know Troy Elliot."

"Here, team," Alex called out, popping the whip over the team. The stage jerked forward, and the driver groaned as the woman tried to ease his pain.

CHAPTER TWELVE

Unaware that someone had just held up a stagecoach claiming to be the Beau Bandito, Troy Elliot was standing at the bar in the Yellow Dog Saloon in Roseburg.

"Hello, cowboy, would you like some company?" one of the percentage girls asked. Like most bar girls, it was difficult to guess how old she was, because rigors of her life tended to make her look older than she actually was. "My name is Roxanne."

"Hello, Roxanne, sure join me. I never pass up the opportunity to spend a few minutes with a pretty young lady. Tell the bartender what you want."

Roxanne held up her finger, and the bartender served her a drink without a word having passed between them.

"What's your name? I don't want to have to call you cowboy all day."

"Cary," Troy said, using the alias he had acquired.

"Cary what?"

Troy chuckled. "Did I ask you for your last name?"

"I guess you've got me there, Cary. You didn't ask for my last name. So, we'll keep it at Cary and Roxanne. All the tables are full, so I hope you don't mind standing on your feet for a while."

"Not at all, I prefer it."

"Of course," she added with a sly smile, "we don't have to stand or sit, if you'd prefer to lie down."

"This is good," Troy said, lifting his beer mug.

Troy didn't notice that a rather short, beady-eyed man seemed to be studying him, nor would he have recognized Angus Depro if he had noticed. Angus left the bar in a rather determined gait.

"I'm tellin' you Dewey, it's him, I know it is," Angus said, sharing the information with a taller, hook-nosed man he met in the Double Eagle Bar, Roseburg's only other saloon.

"How do you know it's him?" Dewey asked.

"'Cause I seen 'im once when me 'n' Eddie 'n' Dusty tried to hold up the stagecoach he was ridin' shotgun on. He told the girl his name was Cary, but he was lyin'. I remember 'im good, 'cause he kilt Eddie 'n' Dusty before I got away."

"They's a fifteen hunnert dollar reward on 'im," Dewey said.

"Onliest thing is, they's a reward out for me too, 'in iffen I was to try 'n' collect a reward for killin' 'im, why they might find out about me."

"There don't no one know me. I'll collect the reward 'n' then we can split it," Dewey offered.

"There ain't goin' to be no reward, lessen we kill 'im," Angus said.

"The problem is, he's faster 'n' greased lightnin' with that gun of hissin'," Dewey said.

"There ain't no need of us facin' 'im down. Hell, he's a wanted man, we can just shoot 'im in the back 'n' it wouldn't make no difference."

"All right, let's go kill the son of a bitch."

Roxanne was laughing at something Troy had just said when there were two shots fired from just inside the door. One of the shots smashed the beer mug Troy was holding, and the other shot hit Roxanne in the forehead.

Troy dropped what remained of his beer mug, turned toward the door as he was drawing his pistol, and he got two shots off, killing Angus and Dewey before either one of them could get off a second shot.

During the immediate outburst of frenzied, shocked, activity, Troy, who had no desire to answer any questions, holstered his pistol and left the saloon. He was well out of town before the sheriff had time to respond to the shooting.

Twenty-six miles south of where Troy was for the moment, the stagecoach was just rolling into Canyonville where it created quite a stir. It was unusual enough to see that the regular driver wasn't handling the team. It was more unusual to see the driver replaced by a woman, especially one as lovely and as elegantly dressed as Alex Pendleton. But the biggest surprise of all was that she demonstrated as much skill as anyone who had ever negotiated the streets with a six-horse hitch. By the time Alex pulled the team to a halt in front of the Wells Fargo office, there were thirty or forty people running alongside to see what had happened.

"We've been robbed!" the drummer shouted, hopping out immediately to try to assume some authority.

"Who did it?" someone in the crowd asked.

"Why, who do you think it was?" the drummer answered. "It was none other than Troy Elliot himself. He was wearin' a flour sack over his head, but I could see those eyes, and I recognized him all right. I've seen him enough times to know."

"Okay, boys," the sheriff said. "Get saddled up. It looks like Elliot pulled off another one."

"We need to get Jesse to the doctor's office, right away," Alex said as she climbed down from the driver's seat. "And it wasn't Troy Elliot."

At the sound of her voice, everyone stopped talking.

"Hello, Alex," the sheriff said. "I saw that was you bringin' in the stage. I thought you were in Denver. And you say it wasn't Troy Elliot?"

"I've come back," Alex said simply. "Sheriff, I don't know who the robber was, but I know who it wasn't. It wasn't Troy Elliot."

"What do you mean, it wasn't Troy Elliot?" the drummer asked. "Little lady, you was probably too upset to be thinkin' right. If you wasn't, you would'a known it was Troy Elliot, by the fact that he give you that trinket like he gives all the ladies."

"Oh," Alex said coolly, "you mean like the one he gave you?" She reached into the drummer's vest pocket and pulled out the locket the bandit had given him.

When the laughter died down the sheriff asked, "Alex, why do you say it wasn't Troy Elliot?"

"Because I know Troy Elliot. The man who robbed us was bigger and had a different voice."

"Well, I know Troy Elliot too," the drummer said. "And I'm sayin' it was him what robbed us."

"I'm inclined to believe the girl," the sheriff said, dismissing the drummer's remarks.

"Why would you take her word over mine?" the drummer asked. "Surely, sir, I'm a reputable source."

"You didn't really know Troy Elliot," the boy accused the drummer. "You was just tellin' me a story."

"Even the kid knows when you're tellin' a tall tale, mister," someone in the crowd said.

The drummer looked at the boy, then squared his hat defiantly on his head. "Have my luggage brought to the hotel," he ordered the station agent, and walked away, followed by the laughter of the crowd.

"Miss Pendleton, I don't know if you remember me, I'm John Coburn," a tall, thin man said, stepping forward from the crowd. "I'm the chief agent for Wells Fargo here in Canyonville, and I want you to know how much we appreciate this. If there is ever anything I can do for you, please let me know."

"Perhaps there will be something, Mr. Coburn," Alex said. "I'd like to talk to you tomorrow if I can."

"Certainly," Coburn answered. "Anytime, anytime. Right now, if you'd like."

"No, now I want a hotel room, a bath and a meal, in that order," Alex said.

"Miss Pendleton, may I take the liberty of reserving a table at seven o'clock? I hope you will be my guest for supper," a new voice broke in.

Alex looked toward the speaker and saw the admiring eyes of Grayson Thornbury.

"Yes," she heard herself answering. "I accept your offer, Mr. Thornbury."

When Alex came down to dinner that evening, Grayson Thornbury was standing by an elegantly laid table in the dining room of the Overland Hotel, waiting to greet her. Alex's brief sojourn in Denver had taught her how to enhance her natural beauty and she made a breathtaking appearance in a gown of golden satin, the skirt of which billowed out in layers like the petals of a yellow rose.

"You are even lovelier than I remembered, my dear," Thornbury said, holding a chair for her. "I do hope you've been able to put the unpleasantness of this afternoon behind you."

"I was relieved to hear that Jesse would survive," Alex said as she sat down. "And I feel much better after my bath."

Grayson looked at her closely, his eyes reflecting his appreciative appraisal of her.

"I must say, Alexandria, that Denver did well by you. Never have I seen such a fantastic blossoming of natural beauty into elegant loveliness. Did you enjoy your stay there?"

"Yes, but I am more than happy to return to Oregon. I missed my mountains."

"What are you going to do now?" Grayson asked.

"Mr. Coburn asked me to stop by and see him. I'm going to tomorrow, and I'm going to ask him for a job. I am badly in need of one."

"Well, I might be able to find something for you," Grayson said. "What sort of job do you want?"

"I want to drive a stagecoach," Alex said.

Grayson laughed.

"Why do you think that's so funny?" Alex flared. "You saw me bring that stage in today. I had to bring it down the side of the mountain—that's as dangerous a pass as anywhere on the line. But I didn't have any trouble with it."

"You're right," Thornbury said. "I had no right to laugh at you. But Alex, look at you now. You look as if you should be the hostess of a gubernatorial reception, and you're talking about driving a stage. The idea is a difficult one to adjust to."

"I can't help it," Alex said. "Gray, it's what I want to do more than anything else in the world. Surely Mr. Coburn wouldn't deny me that chance? Not after what happened to my father...not after what I did for them today?"

"I like it when you call me Gray," Grayson said. He leaned back in his chair and studied Alex for a moment. "I'll tell you what I'll do," he went on. "I'll make you my cause célèbre. I'll plead your case for you, if necessary, all the way to the Wells Fargo front office. Now how will that be?"

"Would you really do that for me?"

"Absolutely," Grayson said. "If that's what you want, that's what I'll do."

"Oh, Gray, do that and I'll forever be in your debt," Alex cried.

"And that's all I want," Grayson replied. He had ordered their dinner in advance, and they dined sumptuously on roast squab, wild rice, peach flambé and chilled champagne. After the meal, Grayson, after asking her permission, lit a cheroot and waved the used dishes away. "Have you a place to stay?" he asked.

"I've taken a room here in the Overland," Alex replied. "It will be fine for the time being."

"A single room? Oh, no, that will never do," Grayson said. "I have a suite of rooms right here which I keep for clients and associates who come to Canyonville. They aren't being used at the moment, so allow me to place them at your disposal."

"Oh, no, I couldn't do that," Alex said. "That wouldn't be proper."

Grayson laughed. "My dear, why is it that I feel that word is artificial, applied to you?"

"Are you suggesting that I'm not proper?" Alex asked

sharply.

"Yes, but not in the sense you are taking it. I'm saying that someone like you can rise above social propriety. You aren't bound by rules, Alex; you're as free as you want to be. The fact that you want to drive a stage proves that. Believe me, I meant it as a compliment. So, what about my offer? I don't live here in the hotel, if that would make you feel better. I have an apartment behind my law office."

"Sure," Alex said. "Why not? That sounds more comfortable than a single room, and right now, I'm interested in something comfortable. In fact, I may just sleep all through tomorrow, I'm that tired."

"Forgive me, Alex, of course you are," Grayson said. "I won't detain you unnecessarily." He took a key from his pocket and held it out for her to see. "It's suite 206, second floor, all the way to the rear of the building. This is the only key I have, so you needn't worry about privacy. I'll have your things moved from your room to the suite now, and then take my leave."

Grayson signaled a waiter, handed him the key and charged him with the instructions. "Now, my dear," he said as the waiter hurried off to see to the matter, "we will just about have time for a nightcap."

"You're too kind, Gray," Alex said. "I don't know how I will ever be able to repay you."

"I'll find a way," Grayson smiled. "Ah, this is an excellent sherry." He held the glass toward Alex. "Enjoy it."

Grayson Thornbury's suite consisted of a bedroom, a sitting room, and to Alex's pleasant surprise, a bathroom. Earlier, she had bathed in the public bathroom, at the end of the hall, and though the door had been locked, she had watched the doorknob intently the whole time, lest someone try to enter and disturb her privacy.

The bed was large and inviting, the quilt was already turned down, and the pillows were fluffed. A kerosene lantern burned low on the bedside table, awaiting only the twist of the wick key to flood the room with bright, golden light.

Alex left the lamp low, preferring to undress in the semi-darkness, and finally, as she slipped in between the cool sheets, she turned the key to snuff the flame entirely. Sleep was upon her in a matter of minutes.

All the restaurants had already closed when Troy rode into Canyonville that night. Hoping he could still get something at the saloon, Troy tied his horse to the hitching rail, then went into the Pair O' Dice saloon. There he learned that he could get a bowl of beef soup, so he ordered it, then found an empty table.

"Huh uh, it warn't neither Troy Elliot what held up the stage. That woman that was drivin' the stage, you know the one, she was Rice Pendleton's daughter, she said it warn't him."

Hearing his name spoken, Troy listened more attentively.

"She sure is a purty thing, I'll say that," one of the others at the table said.

"Yeah, that lawyer feller, Grayson Thornbury, he thinks she's pretty too. He's put her up in his suite at the Overland Hotel."

"Damn, you mean she's spendin' the night with Thornbury?"

"Naw, he ain't stayin' with her, if he was, he'd more 'n likely have her over at his own place. He keeps that hotel suite all the time for important people that come to town."

"What's a suite?"

"It means it's more than one room. It's like a bedroom 'n' a sittin' room."

"How do you know that?"

"My wife works for the Overland Hotel, cleanin' rooms 'n' such. This here suite is on the second floor, 206 it is. A couple of months ago, Joe Sayers stayed in it, 'n' my wife met him."

"Who's Joe Sayers?"

"Damn, Harold, don't you know nothin'? He's the Lieutenant Governor of Texas."

"Here's your soup, sir," a kitchen employee said, putting the bowl down before Troy.

Alex had no idea how long she had been asleep when something awakened her. She sat up abruptly, her senses attuned to whatever had disturbed her. Then she heard it, a faint sound at the window. Curious now, she struck a match to light the lamp. The wick flamed up, illuminating the room, and she swung her feet over the edge of the bed and walked toward the window, dressed only in her nightgown.

It was typical of Alex that she would go toward the sound, rather than away from it, for Alex was a girl of immense courage and unbridled curiosity. Thus, it was that the principal question in her mind was more of who was at her window, than why.

"Who are you, and what do you want?" Alex asked, standing just inside the window.

"Alex, it's me," a voice said. "I want to talk to you."

"Who? Who is it?"

The window shutters were pushed inward, and a man swung from the ledge outside through the open window. There, standing only in the ambient light of the moon, was Troy Elliot.

"Hello, Alex. It's good to see that you have come back. I missed you while you were in Denver."

"You!" Alex gasped. "You have no right to miss me. And what are you doing here in the middle of the night?"

"Would you suggest I come to see you in the middle of the day?" Troy answered. "I'm a wanted man, Alex."

"I certainly do not suggest that, sir. I suggest that you don't come to see me at all! How dare you, after what you have done?"

"That's just it, Alex," Troy said. "I didn't do what you think I did."

"You're lying," Alex said. She saw a water pitcher on the dresser, and she grabbed it and raised it high, preparatory to smashing it down over Troy's head. Troy managed to catch her arm just in time, and he gently removed the pitcher and set it down.

"Alex, you are going to listen to me!" he demanded.

"I am not," she said. "You get out of here right now, or I'll scream."

Alex opened her mouth to scream, and Troy put his hand over it.

"Promise me you won't scream," Troy said.

Alex shook her head in the negative.

"Very well, I shall keep my hand here."

Alex bit him, so Troy pulled off the bandana which he wore around his neck, and quickly, despite Alex's struggles, fashioned a gag. He pushed her over to the bed, then down onto it. He sat on the bed and held her arms pinioned to the sheets. "I said you are going to listen to me, Alex, and I meant it," Troy said again. Finally, Alex stopped struggling, and looked at him with angry, amber eyes.

"That's better," Troy said. "Now, first, I want to

thank you for coming to my defense today. If you hadn't spoken up, there would have been one more robbery attributed to me."

Troy saw the questioning look in Alex's eyes, and he laughed. "I know, you want to know how I found out. I overheard some people talking about it while I was having my supper. But this is an example of what I'm talking about. Everything is blamed on me. If I did as much as people said I did, I'd have to have wings to fly from place to place. I'll admit that I've robbed a few stages, but that's because I have no alternative now. I'm a wanted man. I can't show my face anywhere without someone wanting to shoot me."

Alex lay on the bed, looking up at him. She tried to say something and it came out mumbled.

"I'll take your gag off, if you won't scream," Troy said. He reached down and removed the gag.

"I won't scream," Alex said, after gasping for breath for a moment.

"Alex, all I ask is that you give me a chance to tell my side of the story."

"All right," Alex said. "Let's hear your side of the story. If you didn't kill my father, who did kill him?"

"I don't know," Troy said.

"You don't know? How can you come in here and beg me to hear your side of the story when you don't have a story? What do you mean you don't know? You were there, weren't you?"

"Yes, I was there," Troy said. "But I don't remember a thing about it. One moment your father and I were talking, and the next I was waking up in an abandoned stagecoach. Someone must have hit me from behind, then robbed and killed your father and the passengers while I was unconscious."

"Then why weren't you killed as well?"

"For a very good reason. Whoever did it, wanted the blame to pass onto me. And I must say that their plan has worked well, for now everyone, including you, believes that I did it. As if I could do such a thing."

"But...but it had to be you," she said, her voice now showing the first hint of indecision.

"No, it wasn't me," Troy said. He had noticed the slight change of tone in her voice, and it gave him hope. He relaxed his grip on her shoulders, and sat up, looking into her eyes. "Alex, you do believe me, don't you?"

"I...I don't know what I believe," Alex said. "Grayson Thornbury swears that he saw you do it. Why would he swear such a thing if it wasn't true?"

"There can be two answers to that," Troy said. "He either saw someone else and mistook him for me, because by then I was unconscious and out of the way—or he himself did it."

"No," Alex said, "that I don't believe. Gray couldn't have done such a thing. He's too much of a gentleman."

"Alex, haven't you learned by now, that not everyone with a cultured manner is necessarily a gentleman?"

"I don't know," Alex said. "But it couldn't be Gray."

"Because he tells you it wasn't him?"

"Yes."

"Why can you believe him, but not believe me?"

"I, I don't know. Go away, Troy Elliot. Go away and leave me alone. I don't want to listen to you anymore."

"All right, I'll go. But, Alex, remember this. I was still standing by the coach when the posse came up. I had laid out all the bodies and covered them with a tarp. You've been around stagecoaches all your life. Have you ever heard of a stagecoach robber doing something like that? And if I did steal that ten thousand dollars, why now am I stealing a hundred dollars here, and fifty dollars there? I didn't do it, Alex."

"Please, just go away now."

"All right, I'll go." Then with a smile, blew her a kiss, and climbed back through the window.

CHAPTER THIRTEEN

Alex awakened slowly the next morning, Never, it seemed had sleep been so delicious, or a bed more comfortable.

Then she had the sudden memory of Troy Elliot coming into her room last night. It wasn't a dream, she was certain it wasn't a dream, though there was an almost unreal quality to it. She was puzzled by his strange, nocturnal visit, but she wasn't frightened.

When Alex walked into the dining room for breakfast, she saw Grayson Thornbury sitting at the same table they had dined at last night. He was reading a newspaper and sipping a cup of coffee.

"Miss Pendleton?" a waiter asked, approaching her. "Mr. Thornbury's compliments, ma'am, and he asks if you would join him for breakfast?"

"Very well," Alex said. 'Thank you."

Grayson stood as Alex approached the table, then held her chair as she was seated. "Did you have a pleasant night?" he asked.

For an instant, Alex considered telling him what had happened, but quickly decided that it would only arouse questions; questions that she didn't want to answer.

"I had a most pleasant night, thank you. The bed is very comfortable."

"Keep the suite for as long as you wish," Grayson offered. The waiter brought breakfast at that moment. "I took the liberty of ordering for you; I hope you don't mind."

"No, not at all," Alex replied.

"I've done something else for you too."

"What?"

"I spoke with John Coburn this morning. He's going to give you a job with Wells Fargo."

"Oh, Gray," Alex cried excitely. "Oh, thank you, very much. This is more than I hoped for!"

"Now, wait a minute, wait a minute," Grayson said, holding his hands up toward her as if to dam up some of her enthusiasm. "Wait until you hear all of it."

"All of it? What else is there? I'm going to drive for Wells Fargo!"

"That's just it," Grayson said. "You aren't going to drive."

"I'm not? What am I going to do?"

"You're going to be the station agent, here in Canyonville."

"Why can't I drive?" Alex asked hotly. "Jesse was badly hurt. Surely they need to replace him?"

"Jim Lacy is going to replace Jesse. He's had his application for driver in for a long time. You are going to replace Lacy as the station agent."

"I see," Alex said, dejectedly. "Well, my name has gone on the driver waiting list though, hasn't it?"

"Well, uh, Coburn is a little difficult about that," Grayson said. "But not to worry. I told you I would pursue this matter further, and I shall. I won't stop my efforts, Alex, until you are a driver. Believe me."

"I believe you, Gray, and I thank you for it," Alex said.

"Actually, I'm a little surprised that Coburn even agreed to allow me to be the station agent. That too is supposed to be a man's domain."

"I had to talk a lot to get that job for you," Grayson said. "But, under threat of a lawsuit, he finally agreed."

"But why Canyonville? I know that Cy Cameron would like to come back to Canyonville from Oak Grove way station, so that his daughter, Jenny, can go to school. And, to be honest, I'd rather go back to Oak Grove way station than stay here."

"He chose Canyonville, because as chief agent for the entire Wells Fargo district, he is stationed in Canyonville. And he feels that he can keep an eye on you."

"I see," Alex said, disappointment coloring her voice. "In other words, he intends to run Canyonville himself, and I'm just his assistant."

"That could be his idea," Grayson admitted. "I know that he had not intended to run the operation by himself. I doubt that his plans have changed that much, just because you are going to be there."

"What did he say? How did he take the idea of my working here?"

"As I say, I had to practically force him into it. I think he finally went along with it because he feels you will become disenchanted and quit after a short time. That, I believe, is his ace in the hole."

"He will never get a chance to play that ace," Alex said determinedly, "for I have no intention of quitting that job. In fact, I intend to go over there immediately after breakfast."

"I told him that there was no doubt you would see it through," Grayson said.

"I will quit that job only when I leave to drive a stage."

"And I will persist in my efforts to get you that opportunity," Grayson said. "Now, enough business talk, let's talk of something else."

"What, for example?"

"Well, for example, I would like to see more of you."

Alex laughed. "Mr. Thornbury, you've seen me practically every moment since I returned. Dinner last evening, breakfast this morning..."

"And dinner this evening, I hope," Grayson interrupted. "And I liked it decidedly better when you called me Gray. Besides, if you have dinner with me this evening, I shall throw in a bonus."

"What?"

Grayson slid the newspaper across the table, and pointed to an article. "A theater stock company is coming to town. I thought that after dinner you might enjoy seeing the play."

"Oh, yes, I wouldn't miss that for anything."

"Wonderful," Grayson replied. "Tickets, I understand, are going to be in short supply, so I'll make arrangements the first thing after breakfast."

"Thank you, Gray. That's very considerate of you," Alex said.

"Now, let's have breakfast before it gets cold," Grayson suggested.

Forty-five minutes after breakfast, Alex Pendleton stood in the front room of the Wells Fargo office, waiting patiently for John Coburn to conclude his business with a customer. As she waited, she examined a showbill which advertised the visiting troupe, and looked forward to the evening's entertainment. Alex had accepted Grayson's invitation without a second thought because she very much wanted to see the play, but she realized that such a thing would have been unheard of just six months ago. He wouldn't have asked her, and she wouldn't have accepted.

The customer finally left, and Alex looked at Coburn. He was tall and thin, with sunken cheeks and piercing black eyes. He always wore a black suit, and her first impression of him had been that he was either a preacher or an undertaker. Coburn tried to smile at Alex, but on a face long accustomed to grimness the smile barely came off. Alex, however, gave him the benefit of the doubt and returned his effort with a flashing smile of her own.

"I am really looking forward to working with you, Mr. Coburn. My father always spoke of your dedication and sincerity."

That wasn't quite true, but it wasn't quite a lie. Rice Pendleton had said many a time that John Coburn was a man so involved with petty detail that he nearly lost sight of the big things.

"Well, I—I thank you," John replied. "Uh, won't you come into my office, Miss Pendleton? We can discuss the arrangements there."

Coburn's office was dominated by a large desk and a huge, dark green safe. The logo "Wells Fargo" was printed across the front of the safe in letters of gold, but the letter "g" was missing and could be read only because it was a lighter and cleaner shade of green than the rest of the door.

On the wall there was a calendar which showed the month and year, July, 1881, and a clock which was adjusted to the correct time daily by a telegraph signal from the Wells Fargo office in San Francisco. It was the yardstick by which all the drivers adjusted their own watches. The railroads wanted four standard time zones, but they had not yet been established. There were, in fact, one hundred different railroad times in 1881, and as Wells Fargo had to coordinate much of its activity with the railroad, it was imperative that all Wells Fargo offices had a common time zone in which to convert to the various railroad time charts and tables.

Alex knew about the clock from her father, who, after a run, would adjust the clock at Oak Grove way station to the current driver's watch. Adjusting the clock had been one of Alex's first regular jobs as a small girl, and it was in that way that she had learned to tell time.

"Have a seat," Coburn offered. "I want to be honest with you, Miss Pendleton. While I owe you a great debt of gratitude, I was persuaded to hire you against my better judgment. Let there be no misunderstanding as to my feelings on this matter."

"I appreciate your honesty, Mr. Coburn," Alex replied, coolly. "And I will tell you that I am accepting this job only as an interim position. It is my intention to become a driver."

"That, Miss Pendleton, you will never do," Coburn said. "However, if you apply yourself diligently, it is possible that you will put to rest my fears over hiring you as an assistant agent."

"Assistant agent?"

"Yes, here in Canyonville."

"I was under the impression I was to be the agent."

Coburn removed a pair of wire rim glasses from his pocket, and polished them pointedly, before he slipped them on, pulling the hooks carefully over each ear.

"I will act both as chief agent for the district, and station agent for this station," he explained. "You will function as my assistant."

Alex sighed. "Very well. I know that even if I had been given the title, you would not have given me the responsibility. And I don't want the title if I don't do the work."

"Yes. Well, I see that we understand each other. Now, Miss Pendleton, when would you like to start?"

"I'll start today," Alex said. "Right now, if you wish."

"Excellent." John took down the timetable and shipping charge chart. "Do you know what this is?"

"Yes. I used to accept shipments and issue tickets at Oak Grove. I know how to use that."

"Good. We have a customer out there right now, I see," John said, looking up as the front door opened. "Why don't you take care of him?"

Alex took the well-worn copy of the timetable and the shipping charge book with her and prepared to greet her first customer in her new career.

CHAPTER FOURTEEN

It was a small ranch near the Wilbur House way station. Troy didn't know the people who ran the ranch, but he had seen them back when he was still riding shotgun. He knew that it was a two-person operation, a husband and his wife, both in their sixties, he imagined.

He smelled bacon as he rode by, and he rode up to the house, then dismounted as the man stepped out to meet him.

"Can I help you, young man?" the farmer asked.

Troy took five dollars from his pocket and held it out toward the man. "I smelled breakfast cooking and I'm hungry. I wonder if this would be enough money for you to bring a plate out for me."

The man made a dismissive wave with his hand. "Keep your money, son. And there'll be no plate brought out. You come on in, you'll be sittin' at the table with me 'n' my missus."

Troy learned that the man's name was Enos Stalcup, and his wife's name was Cora. Troy particularly enjoyed the breakfast of bacon, eggs, potatoes, biscuits and coffee, and when he was finished, he pushed his plate back, smiled, and rubbed his stomach.

"Mrs. Stalcup, that's the best breakfast I've had in a long time. You are a wonderful cook."

Cora beamed under the compliment. "Why, thank you, Mr. Stanton."

"I do wish you would let me pay for the meal."

"That's not necessary," Enos said. "We don't charge our guests, and you are our guest."

"Well then, at least let me do something, some sort of chore perhaps? I know you are running this ranch alone, surely you could use help in something."

"Well, I'm goin' to be doin' some fence repair today. If you're serious about wantin' to do somethin' for me, you can help with that."

"I'll be glad to help."

There was a side of Alex's personality that contradicted the high-spirited girl who wanted to be a stagecoach driver. It was a side that not only recognized that she was a woman, but embraced it with joy, and took pride in being beautiful as well. Thus, on those occasions when she really wanted to present the appearance of a cultured and refined lady, such as going to see the play tonight, she could do so, and with great aplomb.

The play was being given in the Opera House, a building which had never seen an opera, but functioned well for dances, lectures, concerts, town meetings, and occasionally a play. Tonight's performance would be by far the most skilled and professional performance ever given in the Canyonville Opera House, and as Alex and Grayson walked from the Overland Hotel to the theatre, they saw that crowds were already overflowing onto the boarded sidewalk in front of the building. There was a commotion at the ticket window as people fought for tickets and offered ridiculous prices for the few remaining. Alex was glad that Grayson had had the foresight to purchase their tickets that morning.

Inside the theatre, the atmosphere was much rowdier than it had been in Denver, and for the first time in her life, Alex felt more sophisticated than those who surrounded her, instead of less. The curtain parted, and a man stepped through. Alex recognized Peter Kuhl, the mayor of Canyonville, who announced the evening's bill, along with mention of the fact that he, as mayor, had arranged to bring the show to town. Finally, Kuhl left the stage, the curtain opened, applause swelled and died, and the play began.

The actress, Ada Rehan, dominated the stage with her presence. She had a radiant beauty which, from behind the footlights, was eminently more powerful than it was in person. Her figure was superb, and her hair shone as if it had captured moonbeams. Though the play was perhaps a bit deep for the unsophisticated appetites of the Westerners, Ada Rehan managed to carry it off with such skill and finesse that as the curtain was lowered for the final time, the audience still responded with thunderous applause.

"Did you enjoy it?" Grayson asked.

"Yes, very much," Alex said. "And you? What did you think of the play?"

Grayson lit a cigar before he answered. "I've enjoyed Miss Rehan's performance before," he said. "It's a pity we couldn't have seen her in some other role."

"But, Gray, Katherine *is* her role! She's become world famous playing that part."

"Ah, yes, I'd forgotten that you acquired culture while you were in Denver," Grayson teased.

"And you? Aren't you cultured? Aren't you a gentleman?"

"Not all gentlemen are cultured," Grayson said.

The statement hit Alex with the impact of a slap in the face. What was it Troy had said last night? Not everyone with a cultured manner is necessarily a gentleman. The similarity of the statements took her breath away.

"Alex, what is it?" Grayson asked, noticing her reaction.

"Nothing," Alex said quickly. "It was just a thought, that's all."

As they returned to the lobby of the hotel, the clerk nodded at Grayson, and Grayson returned a slight wave, then looked at Alex. "I've taken the liberty of having a bottle of chilled champagne delivered to your suite. I hope you will be gracious enough to share it with me."

"You mean entertain you in my room?" Alex asked, her voice displaying surprise that he would suggest such a thing.

"My dear, I have already mentioned that you are above social propriety. The very fact that we are being seen together and you are staying in a suite known to belong to me has already started talk. If I visited you in that room, there would be no greater comment than there is already."

"I don't think one could be above social propriety, and I certainly don't consider myself to be so," she said, rather stiffly.

"Please forgive me, Alex, I hadn't intended my remark to be so superficial. If you would rather I not come to your room, I fully understand your reluctance."

"You may come to my room, Mr. Thornbury," she said quietly.

As Grayson had promised, there was a green bottle of champagne protruding from a silver bucket in which ice had been packed. Two champagne glasses sat on the table next to the bucket, and a white card leaned against a bouquet of brightly colored flowers. The only writing on the card was the engraved name of Grayson Thornbury.

"Oh, Gray, how beautiful!" Alex said. She pulled one of the flowers from the vase to smell it. "These are beautiful. Thank you, that was so thoughtful."

The champagne cork popped, and Grayson poured two glasses of the sparkling liquid. He held one out to Alex.

"Look at the bubbles," Alex said. "They look like stars. There, that one looks like Arcturus."

"Arcturus?"

"My star," Alex said, smiling. "Did you know that stars have names?"

"Yes, I think I read that someplace."

"Gray, tell me—did you actually see Troy Elliot kill my father? You're quite sure it was him? Could you have mistaken someone else for Troy in all the confusion?"

Grayson got a look of surprise on his face.

"Why would you ask me such a question now, after all this time? I assure you, there was no mistake," Grayson said firmly.

"Tell me what happened."

"Alex, are you sure you want to go on with this?"

"Yes," Alex said determinedly.

Grayson sighed. "Very well, I'll tell you what I remember. There were, as you recall, six of us in the coach. Two women and four men, counting myself. Your father stopped the coach when we reached the top of Looking Glass Pass, and told us we could get out for a few minutes while the animals caught their breath."

"Looking Glass Pass is not that difficult a climb," Alex said. "Why did he stop there? He didn't usually stop there."

"I don't know," Grayson said. "Perhaps Elliot forced

him to stop there. Anyway, I walked away from the rest of them over into the rocks away from the road. I won't be indelicate enough to go into the reason why I had to get away from the stage, but it was while I was there that I heard the first shot. I started back on the run but stopped behind a large rock outcropping when I got to the edge of the road, shocked by what I was seeing."

"What was happening?" Alex asked.

"Your father was already slumped across the driver's seat and the passengers were standing outside. Troy Elliot was holding a gun on them."

"Oh, why didn't you shoot him then?"

"Believe me, I've wished a hundred times since then that I could have. But you see, I was unarmed—as was everyone except Troy Elliot himself. The lieutenant's wife, you remember the pretty young, lady? She cried out, 'What are you doing? You're supposed to be protecting us!'"

"And what did Troy say?"

"He laughed at her. 'Don't worry, Miss, where you're going you won't need protection,' he said. And with that, he shot her, then each of the others in turn."

"Oh, how awful," Alex cried, turning away.

"I think he forgot all about me, because he put his gun away and climbed back onto the seat above the money box. I sneaked up behind him, hit him over the head, then ran back to the way station. I was half out of my mind or I would have taken one of the stage horses. I'm afraid, though, that all I could think of was getting out of there and going for help."

"So, there's no way you could have been mistaken, is there?" Alex asked. "It was Troy Elliot."

"It was Troy Elliot," Grayson said. "Why are you doubting it?"

"Because it seems so different from his later jobs," Alex said, not mentioning the time she had spoken with Elliot and heard his protestations of innocence. "He's practically a hero now, did you know that? He's written about in newspapers and dime novels and I heard he's even being portrayed on the stage in St. Louis. He leaves trinkets for the women, robs only the Wells Fargo Company, and never shoots anyone. They are calling him the Robin Hood of the West."

"How can you say he never shot anyone when he shot Jesse just yesterday?"

"I told you, that wasn't Troy Elliot."

"But how can you be sure?" Grayson asked. "Everyone says the bandit wore a mask and admitted to being Troy Elliot."

"That's just it, isn't it?" Alex said. "If he admitted to being Troy Elliot, why would he wear a mask?"

"I suppose you're right," Grayson said slowly. "Anyway, it doesn't mean anything that he hasn't shot anyone for a while. He's living the life of an outlaw now, Alex. Outlaws have no friends, nowhere to turn, and no place to run. His only chance is to have a slight edge, and he has created this image of himself as the people's hero in order to give him that edge. For the time being it serves his purpose to be known as the Robin Hood of the West. But believe me, girl, if it became necessary, he would kill again."

"Yes," Alex said, "I'm afraid you're right." Alex felt dejected, though she shouldn't have, for all evidence did point to Troy being the one who killed her father. But he had been so insistent that somewhere, in the back of her mind, a tiny spark of hope had flared—a hope that by some miracle it hadn't been Troy. Was that hope misplaced?

CHAPTER FIFTEEN

Troy had been with the Stalcups for a week, mending fences, herding cows from one pasture to another, even repairing the roof on the barn. Now he was preparing to leave.

"Young man, you have certainly done a lot of work to pay for that breakfast," Enos said.

"Nonsense," Troy replied with a little laugh. "I've eaten three meals a day while I've been here, something I don't always do when I'm on my own. And, I might add, they were wonderful meals. Mrs. Stalcup is a great cook. I don't think I've even eaten a better cherry pie."

Enos chuckled. "You did seem to enjoy it, Troy."

Troy looked shocked. "What did you call me?"

"I called you Troy. You are Troy Elliot, aren't you? Don't worry, I don't plan to tell anyone."

"Yes, I'm Troy Elliot. But how did you know?"

"Son, I recognized you the first time I saw you. I provide meat and eggs to the Wilbur House way station. I saw you there a few times when you were ridin' as shotgun messenger."

"Enos, I did not kill Rice Pendleton."

"I never thought you did," Enos said.

Troy nodded, then got mounted. He looked down at Enos. "I can't thank you and Mrs. Stalcup enough for this last week. You not only fed me, you gave me peace."

"Nonsense, Troy. You have certainly earned your keep with us."

Troy put his hand on the saddlebag, then smiled. "And thank Mrs. Stalcup for the lunch."

The sound of a shot rolled down the mountainside, picked up resonance, then echoed back from the neighboring mountains. A young man holding a smoking pistol turned and looked at his audience of three with a smile on his face. He had just broken a tossed whiskey bottle with his marksmanship.

"I'd like to see Beau Bandito do that," he said, twisting his mouth on the words Beau Bandito.

The young man was about twenty, dressed in denim jeans and a white, collarless, stained shirt. His chin bristled with irregular patches of beard, and his eyes were like those of a hawk: small, dark, beady, and piercing. He called himself the Texas Kid though, in fact, he had never been to Texas.

"Jasper, why do you worry so much about Troy Elliot?" The man who asked was well dressed, well groomed, and handsome in a dark and sultry way. He was known to the others as Grady.

"I don't worry about him," Jasper said. "He should worry about me. If I ever get a chance to come face to face with him, I'll kill him."

"He's not that easy to kill. I know three men, competent gunman all, who tried to kill him but were themselves, killed in the attempt," Grady said.

"Yeah, I know, you're talking about Watson, McBean, and Condon. I could have, easily, taken either one of 'em."

"But that's just the point, Jasper," Grady said. "Elliot took on all three of them at the same time."

Grady said nothing about being the one who had hired the three men to kill Elliot.

"Yeah, well why do we want to kill the goose that lays the golden eggs, anyway?" The man who asked the question called himself Armstrong. Armstrong and Kimball had only recently joined the group, and the clothes they wore, though now dirty and worn, reflected the style of a city and better times.

"Armstrong's right," Grady said. "We've got to keep Elliot around and keep him active just a little longer."

"Why?" Jasper asked.

"If I explained, you wouldn't understand."

"Try me."

"All right. Soon a railroad is going to be built from Eugene City to Canyonville."

"What does that have to do with keeping Elliot alive?"

"Railroads need money to operate," Grady said. "I have it on pretty good authority that within the next few weeks over a hundred thousand dollars is going to be transferred to the Canyonville Bank."

"And we're going to take that money," Jasper said. "Sure, I can follow that. But what does that have to do with Troy Elliot?"

"It's simple," Grady said patiently. "Right now, every Wells Fargo job is blamed on Elliot. That job will be blamed on him as well if we keep him around. And as long as they are looking for him, they won't be looking for us."

"Yeah, I can see that," Jasper said.

"Good, I'm glad I can count on your cooperation."

"What about the girl?" Jasper asked.

"What girl?" Grady asked.

"You know what girl—the one who knew I wasn't Troy Elliot when I held up the stage."

"Nothing about her. Why do you ask?"

"I mean, I should kill her, shouldn't I?"

"No, I think not."

"You sure? It won't be no trouble now. I could handle it all right."

"Yes, it would be easy for you," Armstrong said. "Women don't fight back, do they? I mean you're the Texas Kid after all and..."

Before Armstrong could finish his statement, Jasper had his gun out with the barrel resting on Armstrong's upper lip, just below his nose. "Well now," he said slowly cocking the gun. The cylinder turned with a metallic click. "We'll just have to see how purty the girls think you are without your nose."

Kimball raised his arm and a small pistol popped into his hand from its concealed position up his sleeve. He put the small gun to Jasper's temple.

"Now put your gun away, Jasper," Kimball said quietly.

Jasper laughed. "Haw! Whatta you think you're goin' to do to me with that little pepperbox?"

"Put a little bullet in your little brain," Kimball answered.

Jasper held his pistol on Armstrong for a moment longer. "I could kill him before you pulled that trigger," he warned Kimball.

"I don't care all that much about him anyway," Kimball said. "But if you drop that hammer on him, I'm goin' to kill you."

"Back off, both of you," Grady said. "If we are going to be successful, we need everyone."

Jasper waited a moment longer, then he eased the hammer down on his gun. "Sure," he said, smiling. "I didn't mean nothin' by it anyway."

"You men are going to have to get along with each other," Grady said, "and stay sober! Jasper, you've been drinking, haven't you?"

"Hell yes, I been drinkin'," Jasper said. "How do you think I got that empty bottle to shoot at?"

"I've warned you about it. Armstrong, where did the bottle come from?"

"I don't know," Armstrong replied, relief evident in his face, now that the gun was no longer under his nose. "He got it somewhere."

"Jasper, when you get drunk, you get mean," Grady went on. "One of these days you're going to kill one of us."

Jasper smiled. "It seems to me that that's your problem."

"And yours," Grady said. This time Grady smiled. "You see, we have an insurance arrangement."

"Insurance? What do you mean?"

"If you kill one of us, those of us who survive will kill you."

"Yeah? What if it's a fair fight?"

"That doesn't matter," Grady said. "It doesn't even matter if it's an accident. If one of us die, then you die."

"Ain't it sweet that you love one another so? Is that love like the Bible says? Or is it somethin' else?" Jasper laughed shrilly.

"I told you," Grady said easily, "it's strictly an insurance policy. So my advice to you is to lay off the booze."

"I gotta drink, or go crazy," Jasper protested. "There ain't nothin' else to do around here."

"I've got something for you to do," Grady said.

"That's more like it," Jasper replied, grinning broadly.

"Yeah," Armstrong said. "I'm getting a little bored myself."

"What is it?" Kimball asked.

"You're going to hit the Canyonville stage tonight. It's carrying five thousand dollars."

"Five thousand? Hey, that's pretty good," Armstrong said. "How do we do it?"

"You two will stay back in the trees, just to cover Jasper in case something goes wrong," Grady said. "Jasper, you're going to play the role of Beau Bandito again, so wear your outfit."

"Right," Jasper answered.

"And I've got a special instruction for you on this job."

"What?"

"I want you to kill the driver."

"You mean the shotgun messenger, don't you?"

"No, I mean the driver. You can shoot the messenger if you have to. But the driver must be killed."

"Why?"

"What difference does it make to you?" Grady asked. "You've killed before."

"Yeah, but I agree with Jasper," Armstrong put in. "Why do you want the driver killed?"

"It has to do with setting up Wells Fargo for the hundred-thousand-dollar shipment," Grady replied. "Believe me, I wouldn't do it if I didn't think it was necessary."

"Grady, I don't think we should do that," Armstrong protested. "I mean, the driver won't have a chance."

"Don't worry about it," Jasper said. "It don't bother me none at all. Fact is, ever one I kill it's like doin' it without them havin' a chance. They cain't nobody beat me anyhow."

"Troy Elliot perhaps?" Armstrong suggested.

Jasper laughed, a short, bitter laugh. "I could take Elliot as easy as I could take either of you. Or, all three of you," he said, taking in Grady as well.

"I should'a pulled the trigger earlier," Kimball said.

"Maybe you should'a," Jasper said, "'cause it was the last chance you're ever goin' to get."

There was a sudden thump as Grady, who had moved behind Jasper, brought the butt of his pistol down on Jasper's head. Jasper fell to the ground like a pole-axed ox.

"I should have realized he'd been drinking too much when I first arrived," he said. "I thought you men were going to keep him away from whiskey."

"He had a bottle hidden somewhere," Armstrong apologized. "He came out here to drink it, and was already drunk before we realized what he was doin'."

"Listen, I don't know about you two," Kimball said. "But I'm scared of this man and I'd just as soon kill him right now."

"We can't," Grady replied. "He's the only one who can make people believe he's Troy Elliot. We need someone who is as fast with a gun as Elliot is."

"Is he that fast?" Kimball asked.

"Who knows?" Grady asked. "But for one third of one hundred thousand dollars, it's worth keeping him around a while longer."

"One third?" Armstrong questioned. "But there are four of us."

Grady smiled broadly. "No, Armstrong, there are only three of us," he said, pointing with long, almost delicate fingers to Armstrong and Kimball. "Young Jasper will remain alive only as long as he is useful to us. After he has served his purpose, I shall arrange his demise, along with that of the real Troy Elliot."

Armstrong and Kimball laughed.

"That sounds good," Armstrong agreed.

"What about him now?" Kimball asked, pointing to the still figure stretched out on the ground.

"Start feeding him coffee when he comes to," Grady ordered. "And keep him away from whiskey. You've got to get him ready for tonight, and keep him ready for any other jobs that come up."

"Right," Armstrong replied.

"In fact," Grady said, "the only reason I brought you two into this deal in the first place was to ride herd on this idiot. Now if you don't think you can do it, let me know and I'll get someone else."

"Don't worry about it anymore," Armstrong said. "You can count on us from now on."

"Good," Grady said. He started back toward his horse. "I've got business in Medford. I'll check in with you later."

Armstrong and Kimball watched Grady ride away. Kimball spoke first. "I don't know, Nate, I'm beginning to think that we should never have left Denver."

"Did you want to stay around there with a reward on your head?"

CHAPTER SIXTEEN

The stage was due in at six o'clock in the evening. There were times when it had been late by as much as three hours, but now it was nearly midnight, and the coach had not yet arrived in Canyonville.

John Coburn, secretly called "Rabbit" by Alex because of the way his nose seemed to twitch when he was worried or disturbed about something, looked up at the wall clock for perhaps the hundredth time. His nose twitched, and he removed his glasses and polished them, then carefully replaced them, putting the hooks over the ears one at a time, and looked again at the clock.

"It could be that Mr. Lacy decided to go back to Oak Grove," Alex suggested.

"Why would he do that?"

"That's a dangerous pass for an inexperienced driver. If for some reason he didn't get away from Oak Grove way station until nearly nightfall, he may have had second thoughts about trying to drive that road in the dark."

"Would you have turned back?" Coburn asked.

"No, I would have brought it on through."

"Then I'm sure Lacy will bring it through."

"Not necessarily," Alex said. "You see, I'm a much better driver than Lacy, and Lacy knows it."

"Mr. Lacy is a qualified driver, Miss Pendleton. Wells Fargo does not entrust the lives of its passengers, or the safety of its consignments, to in-experienced and unqualified drivers."

"I mean to take nothing away from Lacy," Alex said. "There are many drivers who wouldn't want to run that pass at night."

Coburn's nose twitched and he looked at the clock again. It was only one minute later than the last time he looked, and the hands registered seven minutes before midnight.

Suddenly there was a loud banging at the front door. It startled Alex and Coburn, and they jumped. The banging continued.

"Well," Coburn finally said, "see who's at the door."

When Alex opened the door, she saw a big, bearded man standing there, dressed in homespun.

"This here the stagecoach station?" he asked.

"Yes," Alex said. "Who are you?"

"Name's Warner Miller. I got a fella from the stage out in my wagon."

"What fellow?" Coburn asked.

"I got 'im 'bout six, maybe seven hours ago," the man said. "Found 'im on my place. He's hurt pretty bad. He's the onliest one of the whole bunch left alive though."

"What? What are you talking about?" Coburn asked.

"I'm talkin' about a stage wreck, mister," the man said. "Right before sundown the stage come rollin' and tumblin' down the mountainside, landin' right on my spread. Me 'n' the missus went runnin' out there, and I never seen such likes in my life. It was the awfulest thing you ever seed.

OUTLAW JUSTICE | 135

The stage warn't no more'n kindlin' wood. There was three people, two of 'em dead, and this here'n, who's more dead than alive. Even all the horses was killed."

"My God!" Coburn exclaimed.

"I put the other two in my ice house, and hitched up my wagon to bring this fella into town. It took me 'til now to get here, 'cause I come around river road."

"The river road? That took you miles out of the way," Alex said. "As badly as you say this man is hurt, you should have got him here right away."

"Miss, I told you how that stage looked," the man said. "They warn't no way I was gonna try 'n' come over that pass tonight."

"Alex, go get the doctor," Coburn ordered, starting toward the wagon.

"Don't need to do that," the man said. "I dropped my missus off at his office on the way here. I 'spect the doctor'll be here in a moment, now."

Alex followed Coburn and the bearded man out the door and over to the wagon which stood where the stage would be standing, had it arrived. There was a man lying in the back, covered by blankets.

"I made him as comfortable as I could," the bearded man said.

"Who is he?" Coburn asked.

"My name is Jacob Berger," the man said. "I was a passenger on the stage." His voice was muffled and laced with pain.

"What happened, Mr. Berger? How did the stage go over the side?"

"I'm not sure," Berger said. "After the robbery, the shotgun guard tried to bring us in. He took us over the edge, I guess."

"Robbery? What robbery?"

"It was Troy Elliot," the passenger said. "It had to be. He was greased lightning with a gun. There couldn't nobody be that fast except Elliot. He shot the driver."

"He...he shot the driver?" Alex repeated.

"Yes, ma'am," Berger said. "And there weren't no reason for it neither. He just drew 'n' shot 'im in cold blood."

"What about the other passengers?" Coburn asked. "Could any of them still be alive anywhere?"

"No," Berger said. "There weren't but two passengers on the stage, and the other one is back on Mr. Miller's farm."

"I thought Miller said he found two dead passengers."

"No, sir," Miller put in quickly. "I said I found three people, two of 'em dead."

"One of 'em was the shotgun guard," Berger explained. "The other was my business partner, George Starman."

"That means Lacy's still out there," Alex said.

"There were no women or children on board?" Coburn asked.

"No," Berger answered, coughing. "When's the doctor going to get here? My leg's starting to hurt somethin' awful."

"Here he comes now," Alex said, as she looked down the street. The doctor was running, as were fifteen or twenty other people, drawn to the scene by morbid curiosity, and the sheriff, brought by duty.

"How bad is he hurt, Doc?" the sheriff asked as the doctor finished examining Berger.

"I have no way of telling how badly he's busted up inside," the doctor said. "But his leg is broken in two places. He'll never walk normally again."

"Damn that Troy Elliot!" the sheriff said, slamming his fist into his hand "Is there no limit to what he'll do?"

"Sheriff, would you ride back up to the pass and see if

you can find Jim Lacy?" Alex asked. "There's a chance he might still be alive and I'd hate to think of him spending the night out on the road, injured."

"Yes, yes, of course, Alex," the sheriff said. "Would anyone volunteer to go with me?" he asked.

"I'll go with you, Sheriff," a voice called from the darkness, and Alex recognized it as Grayson Thornbury's.

"Thanks, Grayson. Where's your horse?"

"He's at the stable."

"Mine too. Come along, we'll get goin'."

"I'll be right with you, Sheriff," Grayson said. "Alex, are you all right?"

"Yes, I'm fine," Alex said. "When did you get back from your business trip?"

"I didn't get back until late tonight," Grayson said. "I stopped by the hotel but you weren't in."

"I've been down here, waiting for the stage…what time did you make the pass?"

"About an hour after sundown," Grayson said.

"Gray, you may have passed right by poor Lacy, wounded on the side of the road," Alex said.

"If I did, I didn't see anything, Alex," Grayson said. "I'm sorry, but I saw nothing at all out of the ordinary."

"Poor Mr. Lacy," Alex said. "I hope there's a chance that he's still alive."

"God, Alex, that could have been you," Grayson suddenly said. "Listen, I'm not sure you should drive."

"I'm going through with it," Alex said. "Besides, if it had been me, whoever held up the stage might not have shot me."

"Because you are a woman?" Grayson said. "I wouldn't count on that. It looks like Troy Elliot is beginning to get desperate."

"If that was Elliot," Alex said.

"What do you mean, if that was Elliot? Of course, it was," Grayson said. "You heard what the passenger said."

"The passengers were also convinced that the man who robbed the stage I was on was Troy Elliot," Alex said. "But I know that it wasn't. And that robber shot our driver, just as this robber shot Jim Lacy. It could be that they were the same person."

"You got a point there, Alex," the sheriff said. "Come on, Grayson, time's wasting. If there's any chance Lacy is still alive, we need to get on up there as soon as we can."

"All right, Sheriff," Grayson said, starting toward the stable with the sheriff. He looked back over his shoulder. "I'll see you tomorrow, Alex," he called out.

The doctor had the passenger taken back to his office, where a small treatment room and bed was set up. Most of the curious followed the wagon as it pulled Berger to the doctor's office at the opposite end of the street, and Coburn and Alex watched the crowd move down the street, then went back inside.

"There's enough coffee left for us each to have one more cup, Mr. Coburn," Alex said, as she closed the door behind her. "Would you like it?"

Coburn sat in the chair behind his desk and took his glasses off. He pinched the bridge of his twitching nose and squinted his eyes. "Yes, Miss Pendleton. That would be nice, thank you."

Alex poured two cups, then set one of them on the desk in front of him. "Mr. Coburn, what are you going to do about the stage run tomorrow morning?"

"I'm going to have to cancel it, I suppose," he said. "There's nothing I can do."

"Why cancel it? We've three spare stages here, and an

extra team. Besides, the people are depending on us to keep the route open."

"You don't understand," Coburn said. "I'm not cancelling because I want to. I'm cancelling because I have to. I don't have anyone to drive."

"I'll drive," Alex said.

"No."

"Mr. Coburn, you know I'm a capable driver. You need a driver. Why are you so dead set against my taking the job?"

"Because," Coburn said, "it simply isn't done."

"You mean it's never been done before. That doesn't mean it can't be done. Is there anything in the Wells Fargo regulations which specify that the driver must be a man?"

"What? Uh, I'm sure there must be," Coburn said.

"No," Alex replied. "There's nothing at all that say's a woman can't be a driver."

She opened the top left drawer of his desk to pull out a blue-bound book. "Listen," she said, reading from the book. "'District agents shall have the authority to hire drivers as needed. Drivers must be capable, sober, honest, and able to get along with passengers, in order to represent Wells Fargo interests in the best possible manner'." She closed the book triumphantly. "See," she said, "it doesn't say that I have to be a man, only that I be capable, sober, honest, and able to get along with passengers. I meet all those qualifications, Mr. Coburn."

"I don't know," Coburn hedged. "That's assuming a lot, on my own responsibility."

"Responsibility," Alex said. "There's a good word to look at." She flipped through the pages of the book, and again began to read. "'It is the responsibility of all regional, district, and station agents to move the passengers, specie, mail, and freight in as expeditious a manner as possible. When in doubt as to procedure the agent shall keep in mind that this is the priority responsibility for which he is charged'." Again, Alex slammed the book shut. "I think that's pretty clear, isn't it? According to that directive you would be derelict in your duty to cancel tomorrow's run."

Coburn sighed, and once again pinched the bridge of his nose. Finally, he spoke. "Very well, Miss Pendleton. You will take the morning stage run."

"Thank you!" Alex shouted enthusiastically. "Oh, Mr. Coburn, you won't be sorry, I promise you that! Thank you very much!"

In her exuberance Alex kissed Coburn soundly, right on the end of his twitching nose, and he almost smiled.

CHAPTER SEVENTEEN

The stage out of Canyonville was due to leave at six o'clock the next morning but Alex was down at the stable by a little before five, in the pre-dawn gloom. The stable hand had just begun to round up the horses which would make up the team and Alex went to each animal, patted its face, and spoke soothingly to it.

"Give each of them an extra ration of oats," she told the old stable hand. Known only as Jack, the man seldom left the stable, even sleeping and taking his meals there. It was said that Jack knew every horse within a fifty-mile radius but few humans, though he himself was well known. Alex liked him, despite his reputation for crustiness.

"Wells Fargo don't pay for no extra, Miss Pendleton," Jack said.

"I shall pay for the extra," Alex said.

"No need. I already put an extra ration in," Jack said gruffly. "You got any preference on how you want 'em teamed?"

"The two grays will be the lead team," she said. "Then the other four by size, I guess. I've never driven this team, so I don't know how they like to work."

"You sure you can handle this?" Jack asked, throwing part of the harness over his shoulder.

Alex smiled. "Jack, are you going to be like all the others? Of course, I can handle it. I've been handling the ribbons since I was twelve years old."

"Yeah, but you always had your pa with you. Now you're goin' out on your own."

"Trust me," Alex said. "I'll be back after you have them hitched up. I'm going for breakfast now."

The staff and clientele of the Overland Hotel dining room had grown used to seeing Alex take breakfast in the dresses she wore for work in the Wells Fargo office. When she entered the dining room dressed in pants and a shirt, there was a buzz of surprise and wonder.

"Miss Pendleton?" the waiter asked, coming over to her table. "Forgive me for my boldness, but why are you dressed in such a manner?"

"Because I'm driving the stage to Oak Grove way station," Alex answered with a broad smile.

"Excuse me, miss," a well-dressed gentleman at a nearby table interrupted. "Did I understand you to say you were driving the stage to Oak Grove?"

"Yes," Alex said.

"Oh."

"Are you going to be one of my passengers?"

"I...I don't know," the man said. "I may be detained on some additional business."

"Nonsense, Roy," Grayson said, coming into the dining room at that moment. "Your business is concluded and you know it. You can leave on the morning stage."

"Are you sure?" Roy asked. "I mean…"

Grayson laughed. "Come out with it, man. Are you nervous about riding with a woman driver?"

"I suppose so, yes. That stage has to go over Lane Mountain. I've seen the road there. The slightest wrong move and we could be over the edge."

"Precisely why you have no worry with this driver," Grayson said. "Trust me, Roy, she's the best driver on the line. She would have to be better than most or, since she's a woman, they would never let her drive. Surely you can see that."

Roy laughed nervously and laid some coins beside his plate to pay for his breakfast. "All right, Grayson, you've convinced me," he said. "Young lady, I hope he knows what he's talking about."

"I'll be especially careful for you," Alex said. "We leave promptly at six, so don't be late."

"I'll be there...I guess," Roy said.

Laughing, Alex and Grayson watched the nervous passenger leave the dining room.

"Well," Grayson said, "it appears that you have accomplished your objective."

"Yes," Alex said. Her face clouded over. "Though I had no desire to be promoted over Jim Lacy's body. Did you and the sheriff find him all right?"

"Yes," Grayson said. "He was lying right in the middle of the road, dead of a gunshot wound."

"Poor Mr. Lacy," Alex said.

"Alex, please be very careful," Grayson cautioned. "This fellow Elliot is obviously a desperate man who will stop at nothing."

"If it was Elliot."

"How can you possibly have any doubt?"

"Gray, there's something you don't know. Something I haven't told you," Alex stated.

"Oh? What?"

"It's about Troy Elliot. He's come to see me, Gray."

"What? You can't mean that!"

"Yes. He sneaked into my bedroom in the middle of the night."

"I see," Grayson said coldly. "I didn't realize that you were keeping company with the notorious Mr. Elliot. I imagine my attentions toward you must have paled in comparison to the illustrious Beau Bandito."

"No, Gray, you don't see at all," Alex said. "I didn't ask him to come. I didn't welcome his visit. He just showed up."

"For what reason?"

"To protest his innocence," Alex said. "He insists that he didn't kill my father."

"So that's why you questioned me the other night," Grayson said. "You had been listening to Troy Elliot."

"Yes," Alex said.

"I see. And how does Troy Elliot explain the fact that I saw him?"

"He says you were either mistaken, or..."

"Or?"

"Or lying to cover up the fact that you did it yourself."

"And you, Alex? What do you believe?"

"Oh, Gray, I'm so confused. I don't know what to believe."

"Alex," Grayson said calmly. He made a tent with his long, almost delicate fingers. "There is no room for confusion in this question. You either believe me, or you don't believe me. And if you don't believe me, then you must believe that I killed your father and those passengers. Now, do you honestly think I could have done that and have the nerve to pay you court?"

"No," Alex said. "No, I would find that very hard to

believe."

"Then there is no confusion," Grayson concluded, with the logic of a lawyer summing up his case.

"But I have just as much difficulty believing that about Troy Elliot," Alex said quietly.

Grayson sighed, then stood up. He looked at her with an expression on his face which at first looked like anger, but which Alex understood to be hurt. Finally, he turned to go.

"I've got to get over to my office," Grayson said quietly. "And you have to take the stage out. Perhaps I should give you time to consider what we have discussed here. But remember this, Alex. Troy Elliot is a known killer. And the issue is very clear. You either believe me or you believe that criminal. There can be nothing in between."

"Gray, I'm sorry," Alex said. "Of course, I don't believe you killed my father."

Grayson smiled; the same slow smile Alex had seen many times before. "I'm glad you see it that way," he said. "Now, Godspeed, and I'll see you tonight."

When Alex climbed onto the driver's seat of the stage at one minute before six o'clock there was only one passenger ready to board. It was the man she had met at breakfast, called Roy.

"Are you going to go with me?" Alex asked. "Or are you going to wait until the two o'clock stage like the others?"

Roy was not a particularly attractive man, but he had a pleasant face and a winning demeanor about him. He smiled at Alex.

"Miss Pendleton, I'm a traveling salesman, and I reckon I've ridden over every stage route in the Northwest. As a matter of the law of averages some of those drivers had to be poor risks, but I said nothing about it because they were men. If Wells Fargo says you can handle this rig then who am I to argue, just because you are a woman? I know I sure as hell couldn't handle it just because I'm a man. Excuse my language, ma'am; I meant no offense."

"No offense taken," Alex replied, returning Roy's broad smile with one of her own. "Now climb in and make yourself comfortable because I'm about to give you the smoothest ride you've ever had."

The arrival and departure of any stage was enough of an event to bring several people to the Wells Fargo office. The fact that the stage was being driven by a woman, and a very beautiful woman at that, was enough to bring out more than the usual number of curious onlookers, despite the early hour.

"Roy, any last words?" someone from the crowd yelled, and his call was greeted with laughter.

"Goodbye, fellas," Roy replied, waving through the open window of the stage. "I'll see you on my next trip."

"That is, assumin' you survive this trip," the wag called again, and again there was laughter.

"It could be worse, Terrance," Roy replied.

"Oh? How could it be worse?" the jokester shouted back.

"You could be drivin' this thing," Roy said.

This time everyone laughed. Then Alex called to the team and snapped the whip over their heads. The horses swung the stage around and began trotting briskly down the main street of the town, headed for the road which would take them over Lane Mountain.

Most western stages were pulled by four- or six-horse teams. The Canyonville to Oak Grove to Summit Lake run was always pulled by a six-horse hitch because of the elevation of the mountain pass and the steepness of the grade. Therefore, the entrance or exit of one of these stages was a scene of majestic, grandeur. It was a thrilling sight which never failed to halt pedestrians and riders alike, and as she drove the team along the main street, on parade as it were, Alex felt excitement tingling through her.

Later, as the town of Canyonville dropped off behind and below her, Alex found time to think about things. These moments of introspection had been rare lately. As a young girl at Oak Grove way station, she had often spent the lonely hours in meditative contemplation. Her work as an assistant agent with the Canyonville office had precluded the opportunity to engage in much serious thinking. Now, however, with a four-hour run to Oak Grove, she would once again have time to consider events, and put them in their proper perspective.

There had been many things happening in her life in the past months which had not been given their full measure of contemplation. Now, as if filing papers in the Wells Fargo office, Alex began considering those events one at a time, formulating her attitude toward them.

The first and most significant event had been her father's untimely death. Rice Pendleton had been more than a father to her. He had been a friend and a teacher and the long, quiet hours with him at Oak Grove had been happy ones. From Rice she learned to tend animals, love nature, and drive teams. And it had been Rice who augmented her casual education by applying for correspondence courses and insisting that she study them. She loved her father and missed him very much.

And that brought her to the next event. Had she allowed her grief over her father's death to color her judgment with regard to Troy Elliot? Grayson Thornbury insisted that Troy was guilty, but Troy was just as insistent that he wasn't. That meant that it was Grayson's word against Troy's. Why, then, was she so ready to believe Grayson? And if she didn't believe Grayson, did that mean that he was guilty and not Troy? No. That was more than she was willing to accept. Despite Grayson's insistence that Troy did it, Alex was willing to give him the benefit of the doubt and believe that Grayson had made an error in his identification through an honest mistake, not through evil intent.

That is, of course, assuming that Troy was, as he claimed, innocent.

Just why, she asked herself, was she willing to even consider the possibility of Troy's innocence? Was it because she had never given him a chance in her own mind?

Why not? Was she so ready to believe Troy guilty and Grayson innocent that she didn't look for any suggestion to the contrary? These were questions that had never been given substance in her mind but had hung shrouded in the mists of confusion. For example, Grayson Thornbury had told her on that fateful day that the ten thousand dollars had been taken. How had he known the exact amount of money? Such shipments were generally kept secret and he could not have known the exact amount, unless there was some reason for it. Why was he even riding the stage that day? Grayson Thornbury was an excellent horseman who made frequent trips to places all up and down Western Oregon, but, as far as Alex knew, he had never used the stage before or since. Why was that day an exception? And how could he have avoided seeing Jim Lacy's body last night? It was found lying in the middle of the road, there had been a bright moon, and he had supposedly passed through there after the robbery and accident.

But how could he be the guilty one?

CHAPTER EIGHTEEN

The rims of the stage wheels were covered with steel bands, and they rolled over the hard dirt road with a quiet, crunching sound. As the wheels whirled around, dirt adhered to the rims for about half a revolution, then was thrown back in little rooster tails to be carried off by the whispering breeze. The sun was still early-morning low over the mountains, and way down in the valley a morning mist wrapped itself around the Ponderosa pines, clinging to the branches in flowing tendrils of lace as delicate as the finest bridal veil.

Alex rode high on the driver's seat, looking out over the broad backs of the six horses, loving this scene that represented at last the fruition of all her hopes and ambitions. She was driving a stage! She was back where she belonged. This was the purpose for which she was born, and never had she felt such elation.

She was about half an hour out of Canyonville, though that community could still be seen as a cluster of tiny white buildings on the valley floor far below them, when Troy Elliot suddenly dropped down from a rock outcropping, landed lightly on top of the stage, then slipped down onto the seat beside her.

"Oh!" Alex gasped, startled by his sudden appearance. She began to halt the team.

"No," Troy said, "keep it moving."

"What are you doing here?" Alex asked angrily. "And why should I keep the stage going, just because you ordered me to?"

"Your first responsibility is to the safety of your passenger," Troy said easily. "If you stop now, he might try to do something foolish. I wouldn't want him to get hurt."

"I see," Alex said. "And did you come to rob me?" she wanted to know, asking the question in a taunting, mocking voice.

"No," Troy said easily. "I have enough to last me for a while."

"I dare say that you do," Alex said. "The five thousand dollars you got last night should have fattened your coffers quite adequately."

"Five thou... What are you talking about?"

"I suppose you're going to deny having robbed the stage last night, and killing the driver?"

"I am absolutely going to deny it, I just got back from Portland," Troy said. "I saw the stage approaching, and I saw you driving it. I knew nothing about the stage robbery last night."

"Then it goes without saying that you also know nothing about the wreck," Alex said. Still, the tone of her voice was taunting, disbelieving.

"What wreck?"

"After the driver was killed, the shotgun messenger tried to bring the stage in. He went over the edge of the road and was killed, along with one of the passengers."

"God, no, I didn't know that," Troy said. "You said one

of the passengers. Then there were survivors?"

"One," Alex said. "He says you were the robber."

"He's mistaken," Troy said. "I told you, that's not my style. I don't kill people."

"Tell that to my father," Alex said.

Troy sighed. "Alex, as God is my witness, I had nothing to do with that except in my dereliction of duty. I was charged with the safety of your father and the passengers and there I admit that I failed. But that is my only guilt. Since then, I have robbed a few stages, yes, but I have never hurt anyone, and I've kept a very close accounting of the money I've taken. So far, it's been $831.76. That's certainly less than the five thousand dollars you said I took last night. I swear to you I didn't rob that stage."

"Maybe you didn't," Alex admitted.

Troy looked at her with surprise on his face. "You mean you believe me? You're willing to believe that I didn't rob that stage?"

"I didn't say I believe you for certain," Alex replied. "I just said maybe. I know for a fact that you didn't rob the stage I was on, yet if I hadn't been there you would have been blamed for it."

"Then couldn't you believe that I am also innocent of any wrongdoing in your father's death?"

"I don't know..."

"I was framed for that, Alex. Just as I'm being framed for so many other Wells Fargo robberies."

"Who is framing you?" Alex asked. "And why?"

"The why is easy," Troy replied. "So far, whoever it is has gotten ten thousand dollars from your father's stage, five thousand last night, and if the papers are to be believed, a total of at least another five thousand from the other stages. That's twenty thousand dollars, and that's enough of a reason for anyone to want to frame someone else."

"All right, that's the why. Now who?" Alex asked. "Who do you think is doing all this?"

"The who is just as easy for me," Troy said. "But you are going to have a difficult time with it."

"Troy, you aren't going to tell me it's Grayson Thornbury, are you? Because I just don't believe that."

"I'm sorry, Alex," Troy said, "but that is exactly what I am going to tell you."

"Don't forget," Alex reminded him, "I was on one of the stages robbed. I knew that the robber wasn't you, though he tried to convince us that he was—but I also know that it wasn't Grayson Thornbury."

"Then it has to be someone who is working for him," Troy insisted. "Somehow, Thornbury is behind all this. That's the only way I can explain why he would try to convince everyone that I was the one who killed your father and then held up the stage."

"I had this same conversation with Grayson this morning," Alex said.

"And?"

"And he was trying to convince me that you are the one behind it all."

"Trying to convince you?" Troy asked, looking at Alex with an expression of hope, and a suggestion of joy on his face. "Alex, what do you mean he was trying to convince you? You mean it's possible—barely possible—that you might believe me? You are ready to concede that I might be innocent?"

"I don't know," Alex confessed. "Oh, Troy, I want to believe you. But Grayson is so sure he saw you. And then there is the evidence."

"All right, let's talk about the evidence," Troy said, "for I have a few questions of my own, if you're willing to listen."

The road made a hairpin turn and Alex negotiated it with skill, taking a moment before she answered Troy. "I'll listen."

"Consider Grayson Thornbury's story for a moment, will you? He claims that he knocked me out, then went for help. But when he returned with you and the posse, I was still there. Why hadn't I left? If I had just robbed the stage, do you think I would wait around for the posse to return?"

"I don't know," Alex said again. "Maybe you had just come to. Or maybe you were so groggy from the blow that you didn't know what you were doing."

"Then what about the strongbox?"

"The strongbox?"

"Yes. The one with the money."

"Maybe you just took the money and left the strongbox."

"There are a couple of things wrong with that," Troy said. "Three-fourths of that money was in coin. I know, because I watched them count it and put it in the box. Do you have any idea how bulky seventy-five hundred dollars in coin is? There was no way I could have secreted that much on my person. I would have had money bags hanging all over me, but as you remember I had nothing. Also, if I took just the money and left the strongbox, what happened to it? Why hasn't it been found yet?"

"So what does that mean?" Alex asked.

"It means that whoever did do this, took the strongbox with him," Troy said.

"But you say Grayson did it," Alex protested. "You forget, I saw Grayson that morning too. He didn't have the strongbox with him. And if it were as heavy as you say, he wouldn't have carried it away on foot."

"That doesn't mean anything," Troy said. "He probably had confederates working with him."

"Did you see anyone else?"

"No, Alex, I did not. I wish I had. I wish to God I had, for then I would have been much more cautious. Perhaps I would even have been cautious enough to prevent Thornbury from slipping up on me."

"But it couldn't have been Grayson," Alex said. "Oh, Troy, it just couldn't have been. Did you actually see him slip up on you?"

"No," Troy admitted.

"Maybe someone slipped up on the stage after you stopped. He could have climbed up on it, or jumped on the roof, just as you did, without being seen. Then he could have knocked you out, killed the others and taken the money. If he was about your size, Grayson might have mistaken him for you, especially as he fled into the rocks on the side of the road after the stage stopped. Then, if he thought you were the culprit, Grayson sneaked up on you and knocked you out."

"Is that the story he tells?" Troy asked.

"No, he insists it was you. He is adamant that there could be no mistake."

"I didn't do it," Troy said simply.

"Oh, Troy," Alex said, her voice cracking with hope. "Is it possible that you didn't?"

"It's a fact, Alex." Although Troy put a hand on Alex's shoulder, her eyes never left the road until they came to a level stretch. Then she turned to look into his eyes. In that moment, it was if they were windows which opened to his very soul. She looked very, very deep, and saw no deception.

"Believe me," he pleaded, "I'm innocent."

"I...I do believe you," Alex finally said. "The question now is, what are you going to do?"

"Do?"

"About proving your innocence," Alex answered, her eyes back on the road. "Troy, you can't go on living the life of an outlaw forever, you know."

Troy laughed a short, bitter laugh.

"The truth is there's nothing I can do. I hoped against hope to be able to convince you of my innocence, and now I did. But there's scant chance of anyone else believing me—especially with someone hell-bent on making me into the criminal of the century. I have to always be on the lookout, because if I so much as show my face in all but a few places, people will shoot first and ask questions later. The only thing I can do is just stay out of sight."

"Troy, why don't you leave the area?" Alex asked.

"No," Troy answered. "I'm looking for someone. A person named Grady."

"Oh, yes," Alex said. "I remember now. Because of your family's murder."

"Yes, that's why I went to Portland. I heard of a gambler there who fit the description: a well-educated, smooth-talking dandy. They didn't say anything about his hands, but I figured him being a gambler, his hands would have to fit the description."

"His hands?"

"Yes. They are small hands, with long fingers and clean, smoothed off fingernails like a woman's."

"Was the gambler your man?"

"No," Troy said. "That gambler was a foreigner of

some kind. He talked smooth all right, but he talked with an accent. My man is from this part of the country. And I'll find him." He looked at Alex, and the expression of anger and determination that had come to his face left, to be replaced with a smile. "In the meantime, Alex, I shall take great comfort from the fact that you, at least, believe me."

CHAPTER NINETEEN

In less than a month, John Coburn's objections to Alex being a driver dissolved. He went from being an obstacle in her path to being her greatest advocate and promised to "take it to the highest authority" if ordered to dismiss Alex because of her gender. His enthusiasm was well-founded because Alex's trips were always completed on schedule. She was well liked and courteous to her passengers and the number of passengers increased, just to be able to say they had ridden with Wells Fargo's "beautiful lady driver".

There was another reason for Alex's success as a stage-coach driver. Stage robberies, which were occurring at the rate of two a week within other areas of Coburn's respon-sibility, were not happening on Alex's runs. Speculation as to why she was being spared ran rampant, but the most commonly accepted reason was that Beau Bandito was too much of a gentleman to stop a stagecoach that was being driven by a lady driver.

Alex did see Troy, though, and she saw him quite often, for he would drop in on her as he did on her very first trip. In fact, she began looking for him and was sometimes disappointed if a trip went by and he didn't show.

Alex's relationship with Thornbury remained friendly, but proper.

Alex continued to live in the suite at the Overland, though now at her own expense, and she still enjoyed an occasional dinner with Thornbury, or shows, lectures, or lantern projections with him, when such entertainments were available. There were even times when she would take dinner with him in his living quarters behind his law office and listen to him play the piano. He was an excellent pianist, and she liked to watch his long fingers fly over the keyboard. It was as if his hands were designed especially for such a talent, and she marveled at his skill.

Grayson Thornbury was having breakfast with two others at the War Drum restaurant in Medford. There could be no greater contrast between the suave, well-dressed Thornbury, and his two dining companions, Cal Stribbling, and Amos Kahn, both of whom had the appearance of the disreputable, rogues they were.

"Troy Elliot, you say?" Kahn added.

"Yes," Thornbury replied.

"What you got ag'in 'im?"

"I am offering you five hundred dollars apiece to take on the job," Thornbury said. "My grievance with him has nothing to do with you doing the job."

"I've heard of Troy Elliot," Stribbling said. "They say he's quicker 'n greased lightnin'."

"I was led to believe that the two of you had a great deal of proficiency with pistols. I would think that since there are two of you, you would have no difficulty in taking care of Mr. Elliot. And, because he is a wanted man, you wouldn't have any problems with the law."

"So, what you're saying is, there's a thousand dollar

reward out for him, 'n' if we kill 'im, we'll get five hunnert dollars apiece," Kahn said.

Thornbury smiled. "On, no, the reward for Elliot is fifteen hundred dollars. What I'm saying is I will give you an additional one thousand dollars. That means you will split twenty-five hundred dollars."

"How much would that be for each of us?" Stribbling asked.

"One thousand, two hundred, fifty dollars."

Both Kahn and Stribbling smiled, showing yellowed, and in some cases, missing teeth.

"We'll do it," Stribbling said.

Alex was bringing a run into Oak Grove way station and remembering a concert she had attended the night before, had been humming Chopin for most of the drive. The way station would come into view as soon as she rounded the next bend.

She never failed to get a strange feeling at seeing this place which had been her home for so many years, and one of the pleasures she derived from driving was traveling the route which took her to her old homeplace.

As she urged the team into a brisk trot for the final thousand yards, she noticed that the three o'clock stage from Oakland was already there. Curious about why it was there so early, she was nevertheless pleased for her passengers, as it meant that they wouldn't have that long wait until three o'clock in the afternoon to make their connection.

Jenny, the station agent's daughter, met Alex's stage as she pulled in. Jenny was fifteen years old, and Alex saw herself in the pretty young girl, and was secretly flattered by the fact that Jenny saw herself in Alex. Jenny too, wanted to be a coach driver, and seeing Alex succeed had given

Jenny hope for such a future for herself.

"You're twenty minutes early," Jenny said, climbing up the wheel to speak to Alex. Jenny had long, straw-colored hair which she wore in pigtails, and eyes the color of Colorado columbines.

"I'm early?" Alex asked. She pulled the huge braking lever and secured the trace lines to the rung in front of her seat. "What about him? He's about five hours early, isn't he?" She pointed to the other stage.

"Oh, that's not the regular stage. There was only one passenger in that stage, and she knows you. In fact, she said she was going to Canyonville to see you."

"Folks, this is Oak Grove way station," Alex called to her passengers. "You'll change coaches here."

The three men and two women opened the door and climbed down, then began to stretch and work out the kinks from the trip. Alex walked around to the boot of the stage and opened it, then she and Jenny began setting the passengers' luggage out on the ground.

"Did you say she was going to Canyonville, just to see me?" Alex asked.

"Yes," Jenny said. "Oh, Alex, you should see her. She's beautiful, and she's wearing the most beautiful dress I've ever seen. She came from Denver and she says she knows you."

"Denver, you say?" Alex asked, looking toward the house. "Who is she, do you know?"

"Her name is Hannah MacDonald," Jenny said. "Why don't you go on in and talk to her? I'll close up the boot."

"Thanks, Jenny, maybe I will," Alex said.

Oh, Alex thought, why did Hannah have to see her here, like this? She looked at her hands and saw the calluses from driving. She was wearing men's pants and a man's shirt, and an old felt hat to keep the sun out of her eyes. Yes, Hannah would have her laugh all right.

But wait a minute, Alex reasoned. This isn't Denver. Hannah is on my ground now. She'll be as helpless here as I was when I first went to Denver. Alex smiled at the thought, then realized that Hannah must have known that, too. Why then would she subject herself to this? Unless... Good Lord, perhaps something had happened to Aunt Pricilla or Uncle Tobias?

Alex ran the remaining distance to the house she knew so well, jumped lightly onto the front porch, then pushed the door open and walked inside. The passengers she had just brought were getting coffee and making arrangements to continue the journey. Sitting quietly on a bench in the corner was Hannah MacDonald. She smiled at Alex, a wan, hesitant smile.

"Hannah, what is it?" Alex asked quickly. "Are my aunt and uncle all right?"

"Mr. and Mrs. Barnett?" Hannah asked innocently. "Yes, of course."

"Well, I was just surprised...I mean, to see you... Hannah, you didn't really come all this way just to see me, did you?"

"Oh, I'm sorry I caused you to worry about your aunt and uncle," Hannah said. "But yes, I came just to see you."

When Alex had first gone to Denver, her relationship with Hannah hadn't been all that amicable. But once Hannah learned that Alex had no romantic interest in Denis Kennedy, their relationship warmed considerably.

"When I inquired of the station agent if he knew you, he said you were driving the stage," Hannah said. "Are you really?"

"That I am," Alex replied with a smile. "And unless

you've hired that private rig to take you all the way to Canyonville, you'll ride in with me."

"I had hired it for the distance," Hannah said. "But if there is any way I can let it go back I'll be glad to ride with you."

"Just sit there for a moment," Alex said. "I'll take care of it for you."

Alex talked to the station agent and worked out a plan whereby the passengers' fares from Oak Grove to Winchester were paid to Hannah for the use of the private coach, and they were able to cut five hours off the trip. Since the coach had been rented from Wells Fargo in the first place, it all worked out, and no one lost money.

"Papa and I will load the luggage," Jenny said. "You can talk to your friend."

"Thanks, Jenny," Alex replied.

Hannah laughed nervously. "I...I had no idea what to bring to wear, so I'm afraid I brought just about everything. That was one reason I hired a private coach. That, and the fact that I know nothing about the territory out here. I could see myself lost at some out-of-the-way Indian trading post. My, Alex, this is certainly rugged country."

"Perhaps so," Alex agreed, "but it's beautiful."

"It becomes you," Hannah said. "If anything, you are even more beautiful now than you were in Denver. And God knows, I was jealous enough of you in Denver."

"Oh, I'm sure I am," Alex said, laughing. "Look at me—men's pants, shirt, and these hands. I'm a mess."

"I don't think you're a mess," Hannah said. "And neither would Denis."

"How is Denis?"

"He's fine," Hannah said.

"And Gladys and Betsy?"

Hannah looked at the floor for a moment before she answered. "I do have some bad news for you."

"Bad? What is it?"

"I know how much you liked Betsy. Indeed, we all loved her. She was such a dear girl."

"Was?"

Hannah looked up again, and Alex saw tears sliding down her cheeks. "Betsy is dead, Alex. She caught some sort of strange fever and died in a matter of days."

"Oh, no," Alex said softly as she thought of the girl who had been the first to befriend her when she was in Denver. Her eyes filled as quickly as Hannah's had, and Hannah handed her a clean, fresh handkerchief.

"I'm sorry to have to be the one to tell you," she said.

"Betsy helped make Denver more bearable for me," Alex replied.

"She was a much finer person than I was, I'm sorry to say," Hannah said.

"Oh, I was just as bad," Alex replied. "It's all part of the game."

"That's just it," Hannah said. "It was a game. Here, in this magnificent country, all of that doesn't seem real. I can't imagine playing a game out here."

"You can't?" Alex asked, the inflection of her voice rising on the last word. "Then why are you here, Hannah? I mean why are you really here?"

"I'm sorry," Hannah said with a nervous laugh. "I guess you caught me there. In a way, I am playing a game now. At least, sort of a game. But I really have changed, Alex, and I really am sorry for the awful way I acted when you came to Denver, and..." she let the last word hang.

"And?"

"It has to do with Denis."

"What about Denis? He's all right, isn't he?"

"Yes, he's fine." Hannah sighed. "Alex, I won't beat around the bush with you. Denis and I are going to get married."

"Congratulations," Alex said with genuine enthusiasm. "Oh, Aunt Pricilla said that one doesn't congratulate the bride." She put her hand to her mouth.

"In this case perhaps congratulations are in order," Hannah said. "It was no secret from anyone that I had my cap set for Denis."

Alex stood up, then looked back toward Hannah. "Hannah, I consider you and Denis to be very good friends, and Lord knows I have few enough of them. I am very happy for both of you. But you didn't come here just to tell me you and Denis were going to get married, did you?"

"No, not entirely."

"What is it?"

"Alex, you're all loaded up and ready to go," Jenny called from the porch, interrupting before Hannah could answer.

"Do I have any more passengers?" Alex asked.

"One, the schoolmarm. She's waiting by the coach."

CHAPTER TWENTY

The Texas Kid had spoken to no one since arriving at the Pioneer Saloon in Jacksonville. He sat at the end of the bar, nursing his fizz water and lemon, and looked in the mirror at the bar patrons. There were only seven customers in the saloon, one bartender, and a woman in her late thirties who was named Hattie. Hattie was trying to hustle drinks from the customers, but she had little to work with. Age and dissipation lay heavily upon her and made her a caricature of the bar girls Jasper had seen in the Portland saloons.

Jasper signaled the bartender for another fizz water and the bartender complied. Jasper would have preferred something stronger, but he knew his weakness with whiskey. He had a very low tolerance for it, and when he got drunk, he got mean. Three of the twelve people Jasper had killed had been shot while he was mean drunk, and he didn't even recall any of it when he sobered up.

Jasper was talented with a gun. In fact, he believed, and Armstrong and Kimball backed him up, that no one, anywhere, was any faster. And that would include Troy Elliot.

Jasper had an edge that served him well, he liked killing. It was more than the challenge, or the excitement of actually facing death. He actually enjoyed killing, whether in the heat of a battle or in cold blood. And that included the cold-blooded murder of the two women who had been on the first stage he had robbed early in the spring. Jasper had never killed a woman until those two. Grady had set up the robbery, but Jasper did the work. That job netted him a share of ten thousand dollars, but when he thought back on it, it wasn't the money he remembered, it was killing the women.

One of the women, he recalled, had mistaken him for the shotgun guard who was unconscious on the front seat. Jasper hadn't known then who the man was. Now, knowing that the guard had been Troy Elliot—the real Beau Bandito—he regretted not waiting until Elliot regained consciousness so he could face him down.

Beau Bandito, Jasper thought angrily. He was getting sick and tired of hearing about him. Everywhere he went he heard stories of how fast Beau Bandito was, and now, because of Grady's insistence that everything be done in Troy Elliot's name, Beau Bandito's legend was growing. He was helping Troy Elliot build a high-dollar reputation, Jasper thought, and that wasn't fair. The reputation rightly belonged to the Texas Kid, and he longed to hear the name Texas Kid spoken with the same awe and respect as Beau Bandito.

Jasper had assumed the name Texas Kid when he left Wyoming and abandoned his real name. He was hiding from Big Jeb Gibbs, the marshal of Mustard Flat, Wyoming, who had sworn an oath to track Jasper down, no matter where he went. And all because of some pipsqueak of a schoolmaster Jasper had killed during a drunken spree.

There were times when Jasper thought he should stop running and face up to Big Jeb, despite the marshal's reputation. And he did have a reputation equal to that enjoyed by the Earps, Pat Garrett, Bill Hickok, and others. In fact, his life was the stuff from which legends are made, and even Troy Elliot was not as famous as Big Jeb Gibbs. Rumor had it that Big Jeb had once ridden a crooked path. Whatever his past, though, he had taken his role of guardian of the peace to heart, and outlaws gave him a wide berth or fell before his deadly gun. It was said that the man who incurred his wrath would curse his mother for bearing him.

It was funny, Jasper thought. Here he was, anxious to build his reputation, when all he had to do would be to face down Big Jeb Gibbs and his reputation would be assured—or he would be killed. And as Jasper had known Big Jeb all his life, and had seen him in action, he knew what the older man could do.

Perhaps it was a premonition of sorts, or the sixth sense men on the run often develop, but whatever it was, it caused Jasper to glance up at that moment to see a man standing just inside the double swinging doors, looking over toward him. The man was at least six feet, six inches tall, and probably weighed 260 pounds. He had dark, gray-flecked hair, piercing blue eyes, a weather-tanned face, and a scar across one cheek. A well-worn pistol belt was wrapped around his waist and the sheath hung low on his right leg. A .44 stuck out from the holster and the wooden handle of the pistol had a large chip missing.

Jasper gasped, then said, "Hello, Big Jeb." His heart was pounding fiercely, and he made fists of his hands to keep them from shaking.

Big Jeb stepped up to the bar and ordered a whiskey. "Anything for you, Jasper?" he asked.

"Whi...whiskey," Jasper said, having to start the word twice. "And I don't use that name now."

"They tell me you call yourself the Texas Kid," the marshal said.

"That's right."

Big Jeb laughed. "I suppose that's as good a name as any. But it's made it hard to find you."

"I didn't expect to see you here," Jasper said. He drained his whiskey quickly, then signaled for another. The bartender refilled his glass, then started away, but Jasper grabbed the bottle and held it.

"No, I don't reckon you did," Big Jeb said.

"How'd you find me?"

"It don't matter," Big Jeb said. "The point is, I did find you. I got a message for you from your mother. She's worried about you."

"When has she ever not been worried?" Jasper laughed. "That's always been her trouble. She worries too much."

"Your mother's a fine woman."

"Sure, and my dad's a fine man," Jasper replied bitterly.

"He tries to be."

"I suppose I was a disappointment to him."

"A great disappointment."

"I've only tried to make him proud," Jasper said.

"How? By killin'?"

"Like father, like son, they say."

"No," Big Jeb said. "That's not the idea and you know it." He sighed. "I'm gonna have to take you back, you know."

"Not alive, you ain't," Jasper replied. He stepped away from the bar and held his arms out, his right-hand dangling just over the butt of his gun.

Jasper's ominous words caused the others in the bar to dash for the far wall, out of the line of fire. The bartender moved to the opposite end of the bar.

"I might have to kill you to take you back," Big Jeb conceded, "but I will if I have to. I guess that means I'd better get a bite to eat now. I missed my lunch."

"Eat?"

"Yeah." The big man gave Jasper a laconic grin. "You know, killin' always dulls my appetite, so I won't be able to eat later."

"What if I kill you?" Jasper wanted to know.

The grin didn't leave Big Jeb's face. "Then it won't matter, will it? What you got around here to eat?" he asked the bartender.

"Eggs, bacon, some beans," the bartender replied nervously from the other end of the bar.

"That sounds fine. Throw in a cup of coffee, and I'll be sittin' at that table over there," Big Jeb said. He looked over at Jasper. "Care to join me?"

"No," Jasper said nervously. Then, "Why are you houndin' me? You've followed me across Wyoming, Idaho, and Oregon. Why?"

"Because you killed a fine man," Big Jeb said simply.

"I was drunk. I didn't know what I was doin'."

"He's still dead."

"I'm sorry about that."

"Sorry isn't enough."

"Listen, are you crazy? Do you know how many men I've had to kill since then? What the hell difference does one man make?"

"Every man's life is important," Big Jeb said. "Maybe if I'd stopped you earlier, there wouldn't have been any of the others."

The bartender walked over and put a cup of coffee in front of Big Jeb, then quickly stepped back out of the way. Big Jeb thanked him and picked it up.

And then Jasper saw it—Big Jeb's hand was shaking as he held the cup! Why, he's frightened too, Jasper realized. Whether he was afraid that he was about to be killed, or afraid that he was going to have to kill Jasper, it didn't matter. The point was Big Jeb was frightened.

Jasper knew that the opportunity would never be better, and he went for his gun at that moment, yelling at Big Jeb as he did so.

Big Jeb had taken the coffee cup in both hands, and when he saw Jasper start his move, he dropped the cup and dipped his hand to his own gun. He fired a shot off just seconds before Jasper, but at the last minute he had made a decision to try to wound, rather than kill. It was a fatal error.

Jasper felt the bullet pass through his shirt sleeve and burn a brand across his arm. He pulled the trigger and watched the expression on Big Jeb's face change to surprise, then pain, and finally a kind of sadness, as he began to slide down in his chair. A dark red patch of blood began widening on the marshal's shirt, and his gun fell to the floor.

"You shouldn't'a come after me," Jasper said, his voice shaking. "You should'a stayed home where you belonged."

"No," Big Jeb replied, coughing. "You were my responsibility."

"I left your damn town," Jasper said bitterly. "I quit bein' your responsibility then."

Big Jeb coughed up specks of blood. "You could never stop bein' my responsibility," he said. "As long as I was the marshal—and your father—I was responsible for you."

"My God!" a man against the far wall whispered. "He just killed his own father!"

Big Jeb rolled out of the chair onto the floor and lay there, still and quiet. Jasper looked down at him for a moment, then looked at the others. "You all saw it," he said. "Anybody sayin' it wasn't a fair fight?"

"It was fair enough, I reckon," one of the men said.

"Mr. Gibbs," the bartender said.

"Don't call me that," Jasper said.

"But didn't he say he was your father?"

Jasper looked down at the body on the floor. "Yeah," he said. "He was my ole man. But I go by the name of Texas Kid now. When you tell this story, you tell 'em it was the Texas Kid that shot Big Jeb Gibbs." He smiled broadly. "And you tell it good, you hear?"

"Yes, sir," the bartender said. "The Texas Kid."

"How about you others?" Jasper asked, looking at the men and Hattie, who now, cautiously, returned to their seats and nodded in silent agreement.

People had been coming in from the street after the shooting stopped, and by now the saloon was nearly full. Among the newcomers was a newspaper reporter.

"Bartender," Jasper said, smiling broadly, proud of his moment of glory. "Set 'em up for everybody. Folks, drinks are on the Texas Kid."

"Did you see it?" the reporter asked one of the men who had been there.

"Yeah, I seen it. Why the kid there was purt' near as fast as Beau Bandito."

Jasper overheard the comment, then smashed a whiskey bottle down angrily. The babble of excitement stopped, and all eyes turned to him.

"Now get this, everyone," Jasper said. "And get it

straight. My old man, who's lyin' stiff on the floor here, was faster than Troy Elliot ever dreamed of bein'. And I took 'im. Now, if I can take Big Jeb Gibbs, don't you think I could take Beau Bandito?"

"Troy Elliot took on three men at the same time and kilt 'em, right here in this very saloon," the bartender said. "'Course he was passin' hisself off as someone named Stanton, but we all know'd who it was."

"So you seen Elliot, did you?"

"Yeah, I seen 'im."

"Well?" Jasper said, making the bartender nervous with his glare. "Do you think I could take Elliot?"

"Yes, sir," the bartender answered. "I'm certain that you could, sir."

"You're damn right I could take the son of a bitch," Jasper said.

Jasper looked back at the reporter. "Now, you write that in your paper. You write that I kilt Big Jeb Gibbs, 'n' that I challenge Troy Elliot, man to man, anywhere he wants to meet me."

"Yes, sir!" the reporter said, smiling broadly. "Yes, sir, I'll do that and put it in big headlines."

"You put my name first, you understand?" Jasper challenged. "You make it read the Texas Kid challenges Beau Bandito!"

"Yes, sir, I'll do it just like you say," the reporter said.

Jasper took a drink and looked at his father's body again and smiled a satisfied smile. He'd always thought his old man was the fastest there was, but he had beaten him fair and square.

Finally, he said to the room at large, "He was always afraid that he might get killed in some town far away from home, and he was right, 'cause that's just what happened."

Jasper laughed, as if enjoying a tremendous joke. "Only thing is, I bet he never thought it would be his own son who would finally wind up killin' him."

He was still laughing as he walked out of the saloon, and to the shocked patrons of the Pioneer, his laughter sounded like howls from all the hounds of hell.

CHAPTER TWENTY-ONE

When Alex returned from her trip to Oak Grove way station the next day, Hannah was one of her passengers. As soon as she got the coach turned in, she invited Hannah to come down to the Overland Hotel to visit with her.

They stopped in the restaurant for a decanter of coffee, then took it up to Alex's suite.

"You forgot cups," Hannah said.

"I have cups," Alex said. "I have cups, china, silverware and crystal in my suite."

"Oh, my, it must be a wonderful suite."

"It is," Alex said.

In the room, over cups of coffee, Alex and Hannah began to talk. For a while they shared funny stories about things that had happened in Denver.

"Alex, there's something I've been dying to ask you," Hannah said.

"Sure, go ahead."

"Did you go to Chipville to gamble with Denis?"

"Denis told you that?"

"Yes."

"I hope he didn't tell my Aunt Pricilla."

Hannah laughed out loud. "You did go, didn't you?"

Alex smiled. "Yes. And we saw scandalously dressed dancing girls. Of course, when I told my aunt that I had seen a dance, she thought it was ballet and she was perfectly fine with it. I never told her the difference."

Alex and Hannah both laughed.

"Uh, Denis wanted me to ask you something. He said he wanted me to talk to you, and if I have changed my mind about marrying him when I get back, he would understand."

"I don't have any idea what that could be," Alex said with a confused expression on her face.

"He said it had something to do with the way he acted on the way back from Chipville."

Alex let out a sigh of relief. "Oh, that. It was nothing. I'm sure Denis told you, we were stopped by a couple of armed ruffians on our way back. I was able to disarm one of them by using the whip only because he wasn't paying any attention to me because I'm a woman. Then I grabbed the reins and put the team at a gallop, and as the horses were strong, and the buggy light and well-maintained, we managed to get away, none the worse for wear.

"Denis was self-conscious because I was the one who got us out of there," Alex continued.

"He thinks he let you down, and that I might think less of him," Hannah said. "He told me he acted like a coward, and that may have been why you wouldn't marry him. Is that the reason?"

"No, that is not the reason. When he asked me, I knew I didn't love him," Alex said. "And furthermore, he may have considered himself a coward, but he has no reason to think that. Denis was unarmed, the gun was pointed at him, not at me, and there was absolutely nothing he could have done."

Hannah reached over to take Alex's hand. "Thank you for telling me this. I can see why Denis considers you such a very dear friend, and if you will have me, I want to be that kind of friend, as well."

"You already are," Alex said.

The two women visited until quite late that night, then Hannah, just realizing how late it was, stood up. "I'd better find myself a hotel room," she said.

"Nonsense; stay here with me, tonight. I won't even wake you when I leave in the morning.

When Alex returned from her morning run, Coburn asked her if she would take the overnight run as well. Hal Cunningham normally took that one, but his wife had sent a message that he was sick and unable to make it. There was no one else to go, Coburn explained.

Alex rubbed the back of her hand across her forehead and smiled. "All right," she said. "I'll be back, but I need to go to the hotel to take a bath and change clothes."

"Why?" Coburn asked in surprise. "You're just going right out again."

"You don't understand," Alex said. "I hold the thought of that bath in front of me, like a carrot on a stick. It's what gets me through the last three hours, and I'm not going to deny myself that pleasure, even if I do have to go right back out. By the way, who's going to take my six o'clock run in the morning?"

"Hal will," Coburn said. "He'll be okay by then. And when he returns, he'll go right back on his own run. You'll get back to your regular schedule within a couple of days."

"Have Jack take care of changing the team, will you? Tell him I won't be back in time to help. I'll just barely make it for departure. Now, if you'll excuse me, I must hurry."

"Thank you, Alex. You don't know how much I appreciate this."

Alex looked at Coburn and saw that he was genuinely relieved that his problem had been solved. She smiled. "Ahh, I don't mind. After all, you said it. I did want to be a stage driver, and you've got to take some of the bad with the good. You just have Jack take care of the team and you handle the loading, that's all I ask."

Alex thought of the upcoming trip. It was called an overnight run because the stage would arrive at Oak Grove too late to return on the same day. The driver and passengers generally spent the night at the way station, and the passengers went on through the next day while the driver brought the stage back, picking up any new passengers who were going in the opposite direction. The prospect of spending a night at Oak Grove again was actually a pleasant one.

As Alex stepped into the lobby of the Overland Hotel a waiter from the dining room saw her and hurried over to her. "Miss Pendleton, do you wish your usual table for lunch?"

"No, thank you, Sam," Alex replied. Alex had made a habit of taking a light, mid-afternoon lunch, as she didn't eat during the trip. The late lunch usually meant a very late dinner, but that, too, was to Alex's liking.

"You are going right back out?" Sam asked.

"I'm afraid so. Hal's sick."

Sam smothered a cough. "He's intoxicated, you mean," he said. "He goes on these two-day binges from time to time."

Alex smiled at Sam's use of the word "intoxicated". Sam considered his position as a waiter to be the badge of a gentleman and he strove to express that in his choice of words. "Sick or intoxicated, it's all the same," Alex said. "I've got to take his run for him."

"Perhaps you would like lunch sent up to your room?" Sam asked.

"Yes," Alex replied. "Yes, thank you, Sam, that would be nice. Oh, has my guest had lunch?"

"You are speaking of Miss MacDonald?"

"Yes."

"I haven't seen her."

"Then send up lunch for her as well. And if you would, send Donnie up in about five minutes, would you please?"

"Of course, Miss Pendleton," Sam replied.

Alex glanced over into the dining room as she climbed the stairs, but she didn't see anyone she recognized. She was just as glad because she wanted a quiet, leisurely bath, and that meant she would have to get into the tub right away and not waste time talking.

"Oh, good, you're back," Hannah said with a welcoming smile.

"But not for long. I've ordered lunch to be brought up," Alex said. "I hope you don't mind eating up here."

"Why should I mind? I think dining in this beautiful suite would be quite elegant."

Jasper and Armstrong were in the dining room of the Overland Hotel. They had come into town for supplies, but Jasper insisted that they stop to "eat a steak that ain't saddle-broke". After all, he wanted to know, what good was it to have money if they didn't spend it on things like women, whiskey, and steak?

They had just taken their seats when Jasper happened to glance in the mirror and see the reflection of Alex climbing the stairs. She looked familiar to him, but he couldn't place her. She was probably a saloon girl he had spent some time with.

Sam walked back into the restaurant from the lobby, and saw Jasper and Armstrong sitting at the table. He approached them with a practiced smile. "Would you gentlemen care to order?"

"Yeah," Jasper said. "I want the biggest, best steak you got. And you tell the cook that if it's tough, I personally am gonna come into his kitchen and settle accounts with him."

"Our steaks are not tough, sir," Sam replied haughtily, as if offended that anyone would even suggest such a thing.

"That's what they all say," Jasper said. "And I've eaten in better joints than this one."

"I daresay that is difficult to believe," Sam said, taking pleasure in the fact that he considered himself to be cutting this uncouth boor to the quick.

"Yeah, well it's true," Jasper conceded. "But as long as me 'n' you got us an understandin', I'm not gonna worry about my steak."

"That's good, sir."

"I'm not gonna worry," Jasper went on, "'cause I figure you and the cook will do the worryin' for me. Especially seein' as who I am."

"Who are you, sir?"

"I'm the Texas Kid."

"The...Texas...Kid?" Sam repeated, setting each word apart. "Is that supposed to be meaningful, sir?"

Armstrong laughed.

"Are you tryin' to tell me you ain't never heard of the Texas Kid?" Jasper asked in amazement.

"I'm afraid not, sir," Sam replied.

"Where you been, Sam?" a young man asked. He had been busy clearing tables, nearby, and now walked over to their table, drying his hands on his towel and staring at Jasper. "Are you really the Texas Kid?"

"That I am," Jasper replied, beaming now under the recognition.

"Gee, I read all about you in the papers. You shot Big Jeb Gibbs, didn't you?"

"Shot 'im dead," Jasper said, smiling proudly.

The young man finished drying his hands, then stuck one of them out toward Jasper. "I'm awful pleased to meet you, Texas Kid. My name is Donnie Banks."

Donnie's hand hung in mid-air for an awkward moment, then he brought it back.

"Boy, you got a lot to learn," Jasper said. "You never shake hands with a gunfighter."

"Oh, no, I...I guess not," Donnie said sheepishly.

"You see, now that I've killed Big Jeb Gibbs, why there ain't no question at all as to who's the fastest gun around," Jasper went on. "I'm the fastest, and that means the others are gonna come lookin' for me, tryin' to build 'em up a reputation. I can't take no chances on havin' my gun hand tied up by shakin' someone's hand."

"I see," Donnie said.

"My gun hand'll always be free," Jasper said, loudly enough for everyone in the room to hear him. "And I'm ready to take on anyone, at any time."

The others who were in the restaurant either studiously avoided looking at him or observed him only with the greatest of caution lest they do something to provoke him into challenging them to a gunfight.

"Is it true that you challenged Beau Bandito?" Donnie asked. "Or was that just newspaper talk?"

"That's true," Jasper said. "Beau Bandito is a phony, and I aim to prove it. I already have, seein' as how he ain't answered my challenge."

"Donnie, would you run up to Miss Pendleton's room and take her order please?" Sam asked, thankful for an excuse to remove young Donnie from the presence of this gunfighter.

"Is she back yet? I haven't seen her."

"She just went up the stairs," Sam said.

"Isn't she going to come down here and eat at her regular table? I've already put fresh flowers in the vase."

"She is in room 206. You may take the flowers up to her if you wish," Sam said. "And I shall see to your steaks," he added, to Jasper and Armstrong grateful for the opportunity to withdraw from the table.

"So, her name is Pendleton," Armstrong said when they were alone. "I believe that's the name of the girl Grady said might come in helpful later on."

"Yeah, she drives the stage," Jasper said. "Hey—I know her. She was the woman on the stage who told the sheriff I wasn't Beau Bandito. Yeah, she was a pretty thing, all right. Maybe we should pay her a visit."

"No, that could only cause trouble," Armstrong said.

Jasper laughed. "You're afraid of a woman? That's the damnedest thing I ever heard."

Alex had just finished her bath and donned fresh clothes when there was a light knock on the door. When she opened it, she saw Donnie standing there, holding a bouquet.

"These are for you, Miss Pendleton," Donnie said.

"Why thank you, Donnie. They're beautiful, how sweet of you."

"Sam said you and your guest would be eatin' in your room."

"Yes, please. What's on the menu today?"

Donnie smiled. "Meatloaf, boiled potatoes, and gravy."

Alex smiled. "That sounds like more than I want, but I've got a pretty hard drive ahead of me today, so I'll take it."

Alex had to leave immediately after lunch, in order to be on time to take the coach out.

"Hannah, you can consider this suite yours, while I'm gone," Alex said as she stood at the door.

"That is so sweet of you," Hannah said. "Alex—I'm sorry."

"Sorry?"

"I'm sorry I was such an unpleasant person when you first came to Denver."

"That's all forgotten," Alex said.

"You are a sweet person. If I hadn't been such an arrogant twit, we might have been good friends even earlier. It is very much my loss."

Alex smiled. "As I said, that's all forgotten. I'll see you tomorrow."

CHAPTER TWENTY-TWO

When Alex returned to the Wells Fargo depot, she saw the stage standing there with the team already hitched. There were four passengers getting on, if they could be called passengers, for all four were men far into their cups. They were singing raucous songs and passing a couple of bottles around.

"I'm sorry about this," Coburn said. "They're lumberjacks going back to camp. They've been celebrating all afternoon."

"Well," Alex said, "maybe they'll be so drunk that they'll pass out and sleep for the whole trip."

"Maybe they will," Coburn agreed, hopefully.

"Hey, fellas, lookit what we got travelin' with us," one of the passengers called out then. "Little lady, you can sit on my side of the coach."

"Naw, she ain't gonna sit on your side. She's gonna sit on my side."

"If you gentlemen will kindly board, we'll get underway," Alex said.

"Listen to the little lady givin' us orders," the first one said. "Little lady, you're a pretty thing, but you don't give ol' Bucky orders. No one gives ol' Bucky orders," he admonished, waving his finger at her, though barely able to maintain his balance, so besotted was he with drink.

"If you want to reach Oak Grove way station on my stage, you'll do as I say," Alex said. "Now please step into the coach."

"Your stage?" Bucky asked. He looked at the others with surprise on his face. "Well, would you lookit this? Damn if I don't believe she intends to drive this here stage."

"That's exactly what I intend to do."

"I don't ride with no woman stagecoach driver," Bucky said. He looked back at Coburn. "Hey, what is this? Don't you have no other driver?"

"Our regular afternoon driver is ill," Coburn said. "Miss Pendleton is our morning driver, and she's kindly agreed to take this run. She is also our most accomplished driver," he added. "I'm certain you'll enjoy your trip."

"If you've no wish to ride with me you can wait for tomorrow's coach." Alex said. "And believe me, I've no more wish to carry you, than you have to ride with me."

Bucky's traveling companions laughed at him. "I guess she got you told off pretty good there, Buck."

"Come on," one of the others said. "It might be fun to ride with a lady driver."

Bucky looked at Alex, then smiled a lecherous smile. Alex had seen many such smiles in the past and she was pretty adept at gauging their intent. Had he not been so drunk, his was the type of smile that would have put her on her alert. As it was, she figured he would be asleep in a short time and would offer her no trouble.

The four men climbed inside, and Alex shut the door. Their supplies overflowed the ox-hide boot, and the surplus was lashed down on top of the coach. The stage was heavily loaded, and Alex knew that the horses would be getting quite a workout on this trip, so she walked along the hitch, speaking soothingly to each of them. Finally, she returned and started climbing up to the driver's seat.

"I put the mail bag under the seat," Coburn said. "At least you don't have to worry about any money tonight. Just a few letters."

"That's good," Alex said, taking the reins in her hand. "I'll see you tomorrow, but only to turn this stage back in. After that I'm going to take the whole day off."

"You will have earned it," Coburn assured her. Alex snapped the lines and the horses leaned into their harness. She pulled them around and the stage made a wide U-turn in the street in front of the Wells Fargo depot, then rolled past the outskirts of town at a fairly good clip.

For the first few minutes, Alex could hear the cacophony which the four drunks passed off as song. But, as she had figured, it didn't last long, and on the flat, straight stretches of the road where the stage rolled smoothly and quietly, she could even hear snatches of snoring. She set the pace for an uneventful trip.

It was nearly two hours later when she reached the pullout and brought the team to a halt to allow them to catch their breath from the long climb. She tied the lines off, then climbed down and stretched her legs and looked into the coach. The four men were sleeping in various positions, mouths open and spittle drooling. It was a most unattractive sight and she decided to let them be, rather than inform them of the rest stop.

Alex felt her own need for the stop, and she walked off the road and along a path through the rocks to a spot which she knew would provide her with privacy. She took the bullwhip with her, the one she used to control the team, because although she had yet to see a snake during one of these stops, she felt safer if prepared for one.

Alex was an expert with the whip, and she used it liberally on the teams without ever inflicting actual pain. She could pop it with the report of a pistol shot, placing it by the ear of whichever animal needed attention, and if a greater impression were needed, she could cause the end of it to snap against the animal's flesh with an attention-getting sting, though falling far short of brutality. It was this expertise with a whip which would allow her to pop the head off a rattler, should the occasion ever present itself, so she always carried it with her when she left the road.

Alex found a private spot and had already started back when she saw Bucky, leering from his vantage point in the middle of the path. She gasped, and her face burned red in embarrassment.

"What are you doing here?" she asked.

"I came to make you a little proposition," Bucky said. "I'm willin' to pay for a little fun."

"What? Get out of here! How dare you follow me down here?"

"Now come on, honey, don't get so huffy. I mean after all, you're drivin' a stagecoach, ain't ya'? That's not exactly a schoolmarm's job, is it? You know what it's all about. I'll bet you entertain your passengers all the time when the price is right. Well, honey, I got me a terrible need, and I'm willin' to meet the right price. You just tell me what it is."

Bucky began opening his pants and walking toward her.

"I told you to get away from me," Alex said. She took a hesitant step backwards.

"Come on, honey, what are you worried about? My pards are dead to the world. Why, they're sleepin' so hard, you'll prob'ly have to pour water on 'em to wake 'em up when we get to the way station. But me, why, I'm ready for a little fun." Bucky suddenly lunged for her, and Alex, having seen him staggering around when he got onto the stage, was surprised by his quickness. She twisted away quickly, darted around him, then started back up the path toward the stage.

"Come back here, you little bitch!" he called. "Who do you think you are?"

Alex ran along the path until she reached the turnout where the stage stood. Then with enough room to work, she turned and faced Bucky, holding her whip poised above her. "Stop right there," she called.

Bucky stopped, then laughed. "What do you think you can do with that little ol' switch?" he called. He took another step forward, and Alex flipped the whip out, snapping it painfully but not severely across his shin.

"Hey!" he cried out. "Put that thing down, slut, and I promise I'll go easy with you."

He took another step, and this time Alex snapped the whip just across his chest.

"Now cut that out!" Bucky bellowed. He grabbed for his gun, but it was no sooner out of its holster than she snapped it out of his hand, sending it careening toward the nearby rocks. He let out a sharp exclamation of pain and grabbed his wrist.

"If you take one more step toward me, I'll fix you so that you'll never be interested in any woman again," Alex said quietly.

"What are you a sayin'?" Bucky asked, much of the wind taken out of his sails. "You couldn't do that."

"If I can hit your belt buckle, I can hit anything I want," Alex replied. She threw the whip out again, and the tip of it snapped against the man's belt buckle. "Do you doubt that I can hit you any place I want?"

"No!" Bucky cried, covering himself now with his hands, crouching in fear before her. "I believe you."

"Then get back on the stage," Alex said.

"I'm goin', I'm goin'," he whimpered, scampering for the stage, holding his arms out to ward off any further blows.

Alex couldn't resist popping the whip with a pistol-like report just by his ear as he climbed back into the stage. The others had snored through it all.

By the time Alex returned to the driver's seat she was smiling. She had come face to face with the thing which had always bothered her. How, she had often wondered, would she handle a male passenger who might become mean? Well, she met that challenge today, and she believed she had overcome it.

Dirty gray piles of clouds began stacking up over the mountains, and Alex knew they would collect enough rain to cascade through the canyons and fill the washes. It was good that she was on the last leg of the trip, because these roads were dangerous at any time, but much more so in the rain, and extremely hazardous in the rain at night. And it would be dark before Oak Grove way station was reached.

The sun began dying in a brilliant display of color, and the dark blue of the eastern sky moved across the heavens, as if pulling a shade down over the world. Soon the last vestige of the sunset was gone, and the night turned black. The evening breeze carried moisture in its breath, and Alex knew that it would be a race as to whether they reached Oak Grove before the rain reached them. She quickened the pace of the animals, and then gave a sigh of relief when she saw the rock formation she used as a sign of when to blow the trumpet.

Alex gave a few bleats on the trumpet and looked through the darkness to try to pick out the cluster of buildings that was Oak Grove. By the light of day, she knew they would be clearly visible from here. Now she had only the golden points of light to guide her.

The rain hit in the last five hundred yards, but by then the worst of the road was behind her, and she kept up the pace of the team so that one minute later she was braking the coach to a stop in front of the way station.

"All right," she called out, as she hopped down from the seat. "We're here. Everyone inside, you'll have to make arrangements for the night."

When Alex went inside, she saw the surprised look on Jenny's face "What are you doing here?"

"Hal's sick," Alex said. "I had to take his run."

"Oh, no, how are we going to handle this?" Jenny asked.

"Handle what?"

"I mean, where are you going to sleep?" Jenny asked. "The other stage has six passengers, and all the beds are taken—in fact, they're doubled up. I thought Hal would be here, so he was going to sleep with Pa. I've already got two other women with me."

"Don't worry about it," Alex said. "I'll sleep in the barn."

"Oh, no, I don't want you to have to do that."

Alex laughed. "You'd be surprised at the number of times I've done that in the past. I don't mind, really, I don't. The barn is very dry and sort of cozy. I'll be fine there."

"Why don't you take my place and I'll sleep in the barn?" Jenny offered, genuinely concerned over Alex's well-being.

"No, thank you," Alex said. "I used to live here, remember? I know what it's like to share your bed with passengers. Believe me, if I'm going to drive back tomorrow, I'd better get a good night's rest, and I can do that better alone in the barn. Besides, unless things have changed drastically around here, you're going to have to get up early and fix breakfast. I know I always had to."

"Nothing has changed, that's for sure," Jenny said, making a funny face for Alex.

"I thought so. Well, we all have to start somewhere, and that's where I started too. Now, if you'll find a pillow and a blanket for me, I'll get along perfectly."

"Do you want supper?"

"Uhmm, absolutely," Alex said. "I'm starved. And I don't get a chance to eat your cooking that often, so I intend to take this opportunity. Tell me, what are we having?"

"Stagecoach stew," Jenny said.

"It would be," Alex replied, making a face. Stagecoach stew was the common term for leftover hash. It was the most universally served, and the most thoroughly cursed, food along any of the Wells Fargo routes. But the Wells Fargo fare budget dictated that it be served often.

Jenny laughed. "I was teasing. Tonight, we're having roast beef."

"Roast beef? Now that's more like it," Alex said. "I'll be right back in after I've stabled and fed the team. And if you let the passengers eat all of it before I get back, I'm going to eat yours," she teased.

"I'll hold enough back for both of us," Jenny promised. "And we'll eat together."

After Alex helped unhitch the team, she led the horses into the barn where she fed them, then stabled them. She looked around to see that there was a stall with fresh hay for her own bedroll, found a nice dry one, then returned to the main house for her meal.

Jenny's father, the driver of the other stage, and the passengers were still sitting around the great table, having just finished their meal. There were two plates set at the small kitchen table for Jenny and Alex, and a crackling wood fire in the cooking stove, which made a comfortable addition to this wet, cool evening.

"Now, isn't this nice?" Jenny asked. "Just the two of us."

"Yes, it is," Alex said. She poured herself a cup of coffee, then sat down.

"It just isn't fair," Jenny said a moment later.

"What? What isn't fair?" Alex replied, surprised by the pronouncement.

"'The railroad," Jenny said. "They are going to have the railroad built from Medford all the way to Canyonville before I'm ever old enough to drive the stage."

Alex laughed. "This isn't the only stage route, you know."

"I know it isn't. But it's the one you have, and I wanted to be just like you."

"Well, don't forget—when the railroad is built, I'll have to find another route for myself as well."

"Yes, that's right, isn't it?" A smile brightened Jenny's face. "Maybe it will work out after all. Oh, Alex, you've no idea how much I want to drive a stagecoach. I want it more than anything, but nobody can understand that, except maybe you. Do you think I'm crazy?"

"Yes," Alex said, "I think you're crazy."

"Really? But you're doing it."

"I know," Alex said. She smiled broadly at Jenny. "But I'm crazy too."

Jenny laughed.

That night, after she had eaten and talked for a while with Jenny, Alex donned a waterproof poncho, took the blanket and pillow, and darted through the rain to the barn, there to make her bed. The stall she had selected proved to be an excellent choice as it was dry and warm despite the rain, and the straw was fresh and pleasant smelling.

After her bed was made Alex walked over to the side of the barn and peered out through a window to look at the streaks of rain slash down out of the night sky and watch the flashes of lightning illuminate the range of mountains across the valley. After each lightning flash she heard the thunder roll, and after one particularly loud burst of thunder she heard the horses move about restlessly. She spoke soothingly to them to reassure them.

As she stood in the window some of the rain blew into her face, but she made no attempt to escape. She loved the rain. It blanketed all sight and sound and formed a curtain behind which her soul could exist in absolute solitude. Only those with whom she really wanted to share could penetrate it.

The door to the barn opened and closed, but Alex didn't look around. "Jenny, are you still worrying about me?" she asked.

"I'm not Jenny, but I do worry about you," a man's voice answered.

Alex turned quickly. "Troy, what are you doing here?"

"I'm getting in out of the rain," Troy said. "What are you doing here? I thought you only took the morning runs."

Alex explained about Hal's illness and the arrangement she had made with Coburn. Then she asked, "What do you mean you are getting out of the rain? You mean you come here often?"

Troy gave a sheepish grin. "Yeah, I do," he said. "I have

to stay somewhere, and I sort of like it here. It was here that I first met you if you remember."

"But isn't it dangerous for you?"

"Everywhere is dangerous for me now," Troy said. "So, I might as well find a place that is comfortable, and that I like."

"Why hasn't anyone ever discovered you here? One of the drivers, or someone who is tending the horses?"

"Come up here, I'll show you," Troy said.

Alex followed Troy across the floor of the barn, then up a ladder to the hayloft. Once there, Troy moved a couple of bales of hay, then held his arm out invitingly.

"This is where I live. Would you like to take a look around?"

Alex hesitated, and Troy stepped back, then half raised his hands.

"I assure you, I'll be the perfect gentleman," he said.

"Yes, all right, then in that case, I would love to see it."

Alex had to bend over to walk through the space, but once inside it was pitch dark, and she could sense that she was in a large cavern-like area. "I'll light a lantern as soon as I close the door," Troy said, pulling the bales of hay back to conceal the entrance. "Now, from out there it looks just like a stack of hay. But from in here..." Troy let the sentence hang as he struck a match to a lantern.

A golden light flared out from the lamp, and Alex was able to look around her. Troy had ingeniously constructed a room from the bales of hay, complete with a bed made by stretching blankets over straw, a small table, a wash basin, and even a few changes of clothes.

"You aren't just staying here, temporarily, are you? You actually live here, don't you?" Alex said, fascinated by her surroundings.

"Yes," Troy said. He pulled a loose board out from the wall. "I bank here too," he added with a smile. "This is where I keep my ill-gotten gains."

Alex looked down inside and saw a small sack.

"Count it," Troy said.

"What?"

"Go ahead. Count it. It'll prove to you that I've taken only a few dollars here and there, and not the thousands of dollars I am being accused of taking."

Alex laughed. "I don't need to count it," she said. "The fact that you were willing to let me count it is proof enough...if I still needed proof."

"You mean you don't?"

"No," Alex said easily. "I don't need proof anymore."

CHAPTER TWENTY-THREE

Armstrong had tried to keep the Texas Kid from drinking too much, but despite his efforts, Jasper spent the entire afternoon drinking. When Jasper was determined to do something, there was very little that Armstrong, or anyone else for that matter, could do to stop him. Especially as Jasper had told him in no uncertain terms that one more comment about his drinking would be all the excuse he needed to close Armstrong's mouth forever.

So, under Armstrong's watchful but impotent charge, Jasper drank heavily, grew intoxicated, and Armstrong walked on eggshells to keep from saying or doing anything that would set off the volatile young man. Thus, it was that when Jasper suggested they spend the night in town rather than return to their mountain camp through the rain, Armstrong readily agreed.

The rain began just after nightfall and by the time Jasper and Armstrong left the saloon, leaving only because it had closed for the night, it was falling in a deluge. Armstrong suggested that they bunk down in the livery stable with their horses, but Jasper wouldn't hear of it.

"We got money, we'll stay in the hotel."

"But it's so late, Jasper," Armstrong protested. "The clerk's probably gone to bed already."

"Then we'll get his ass up," Jasper said. "That's what night clerks in a hotel do."

Jasper took another swallow of the bottle he had brought with him. "Come on, let's do this in style."

Jasper didn't wait for an answer. He lunged straight toward the hotel, nearly falling off the boardwalk into the mud of the street, then lurched through the driving downpour, staggered across the street and onto the boarded walk that was in front of the hotel.

Armstrong ran after him, wishing that Kimball and Grady were here to help him control this idiot, wishing also that he had the courage to just shoot the son of a bitch in the back and get it over with.

The clock over the bar had said two o'clock when they finally left the saloon, so Armstrong wouldn't have been surprised if the front door to the hotel had been locked. But it wasn't, and Jasper pushed it open, then stepped into the lobby with Armstrong right behind him.

A kerosene lantern stood on the front desk its flame turned low to emit only a very subdued glow. There were no other lights in the lobby, but the sofa, chairs, and tables were revealed in stark black and harsh white by the frequent streaks of lightning which flashed through the windows, as bright as the magnesium flares in a photographer's flash.

Jasper stumbled into a table, then angrily shoved it to one side. He walked over to the desk and banged his hand down on the little bell. There was no response to his summons.

"Let's go on back to the stable," Armstrong suggested.

"Hell no. Why sleep in wet hay when we can sleep in a

dry bed?" Jasper replied. He banged the bell again. "Hey, you!" he shouted. "Get your ass out here!"

There was no answer.

"I said get your ass out here before I start shootin' up the damn place!" He banged the bell again.

A door opened from a room just behind the desk. A man who had obviously been asleep emerged, placing his glasses on his nose carefully. He was wearing a long nightshirt and a nightcap, the tassel of which dangled across one shoulder.

"I'm sorry, sir," the clerk said. "I was sleeping."

"Yeah, well that's what we want to do," Jasper said. "Give my partner and me a couple of rooms," Jasper demanded.

"I have only one room left, I'm afraid. You'll have to share it."

"That'll be all right," Jasper said. "Give me the key."

"You'll have to register first, sir," the clerk said. "And the rate is seventy-five cents, in advance."

Jasper slapped the money on the counter, then spun the book around. He picked up a pencil stub, wet it with his tongue, then very laboriously printed 'the texas ked', disdaining capitals and misspelling the word kid.

He also saw that Alex Pendleton was in room 206. She had been on his mind, ever since he had encountered her when he robbed the coach as Beau Bandito. Then, as they had walked through the hotel lobby on the way to the dining room earlier today, he had seen her go upstairs. She was there now.

"All right, Armstrong, I took care of it, let's go," Jasper said.

"Gentlemen, your room number is 203," the clerk said, handing Jasper a key. "Please remove your boots before you go to bed," he added, noticing the mud tracks the two men were leaving on the floor as they started for the stairs.

Jasper lurched about on the stairs, once falling against the wall, but they finally made it to the next floor, then found their room. Jasper couldn't fit the key in the lock, so Armstrong took the key from him and tried himself. As Armstrong was unlocking the door, Jasper tipped the bottle up for another long swallow of whiskey.

"There it is," Armstrong said, finally turning the key. He opened the door and pushed it open. It smelled musty. "Whew," Armstrong said. "We would have been better off in the barn." Armstrong felt his way to a table, found a matchbox, and lit the lamp. There was only one bed in the room, along with the bedside table, a chair, a dresser, a water pitcher and a basin.

"We're goin' to have to share the bed," Armstrong said. "Which side do you want?"

Jasper walked over to the chair and plopped down without a word. He took another drink from his bottle.

"You don't have a choice?" Armstrong asked. "Then I'll take the side next to the wall. I'm goin' to hit the sack now and that way you won't have to crawl over me."

Jasper took another swallow but said nothing.

Armstrong sat on the edge of the bed and removed his boots, dropping them one by one at the foot of the bed. He rubbed his feet and sighed. "Damn, there's nothin' that feels better than takin' off your boots."

"Nah, bein' with a woman feels better," Jasper said, thinking of the Pendleton woman.

"Are you comin' to bed?" Armstrong wanted to know.

"Yeah, in a little while," Jasper said. "I wanna finish my bottle, but. I gotta take a leak."

"You can just go out the window," Armstrong said.

"Ain't this hotel got one of them indoor outhouses?"

"Yes, but it's way down the hall. It'd be a lot easier to just go out the window."

"Uh, uh," Jasper said. "I don't get a chance to use one of them indoor outhouses all that much. I'm gonna use it."

Armstrong chuckled. "Suit yourself," he said. "Mind if I turn out the light?"

"Nah, go ahead," Jasper said.

Armstrong reached over to the lantern key and twisted it. The flame was snuffed, and the room grew dark.

Jasper sat in his chair for a few more minutes, drinking his whiskey and listening to Armstrong breathe. After a few moments Armstrong's breathing changed to snores, and Jasper knew that he was asleep.

He drained the rest of the whiskey, then walked over to the window. He opened the window and tossed the bottle outside, barely hearing the tinkle of glass as it shattered below. He then started to relieve himself through the window, but remembered the bathroom, so he closed the window and stepped out into the hall.

As Jasper walked down the hall, he was so drunk that he was having difficulty staying erect. He supported himself by holding his hand against the wall. When he reached the bathroom, he left the door open as he relieved himself, without concern as to whether or not he could be seen.

When Jasper left the bathroom a moment later, he walked by room 206, and remembered that this was Alex Pendleton's room. This was the bitch who told the sheriff that he wasn't Troy Elliot.

He stared at the door for a long moment. The chances were that the door was locked, and if it were locked, he couldn't get in without breaking it down. He knew that would be so noisy that it would bring everyone in the hotel down on him.

Jasper started to leave, but on impulse, tried the doorknob.

It was unlocked!

Jasper stepped inside and closed the door behind him. He was quiet for a moment, listening for the girl's breathing. A flash of lightning illuminated the room and Jasper saw with some surprise that there was no bed. What kind of room was this? Another flash showed some doors leading off the room and Jasper suddenly realized that this was more than just a regular hotel room.

The last lightning flash had revealed a table lamp and matchbox. Jasper lit the lamp and looked around. There were two doors leading off this room, which appeared to be some sort of sitting room or parlor. Jasper walked over and opened one of the doors cautiously. It was a bathroom. Here in the same room was a bathroom. Jasper had never seen such a sight and he stared at it in awe for a few moments. Then he remembered why he was here, closed the door and backed out into the sitting room again.

There was only one door left and Jasper knew that the girl had to be in there. He opened it quietly and looked inside.

There she was, on the bed.

Jasper stood in the doorway for a moment, listening to her breathe. He walked over to the bed and looked down at her. Her face was in shadow and he could see very little of it, but that didn't matter.

The palms of his hands were sweating, and he picked up the spare pillow, and when he shoved it down onto her face, he felt his heart pounding violently. The girl tried to scream but the scream was muffled by the pillow. She pushed at the bedclothes, but she was so well covered that the blankets worked almost as a restraint and her fighting was ineffectual.

He held the pillow over her long after she stopped, then stood up, looked down at the still body with the pillow over its face. He was struck with a macabre sense of humor.

"You won't be tellin' nobody whether it was Beau Bandito or the Texas Kid what kilt you now, will you?"

Armstrong was still asleep when Jasper returned the room, so Jasper just stretched out on the bed beside him, still wearing his pants and boots, and fell into a drunken, exhausted slumber.

When Troy awakened in the way station barn the next morning, he could tell by the cracks between the board wall, that it was still dark outside. He was glad that he could no longer hear it raining, because riding in the rain wasn't a pleasant experience.

Getting dressed, Troy climbed down the ladder from the loft, then walked over to the stall where he knew Alex was sleeping. He could hear her measured breathing, and he went over to her, then bent down to kiss her on the forehead.

"What?" Alex said, waking in a start.

"I'm sorry," Troy said. "I didn't want to wake you. I just wanted to tell you goodbye."

"Well, if you're going to give me a goodbye kiss, make it a proper goodbye kiss," Alex said. "Not just a peck on the forehead."

"How's this for a goodbye kiss?" Troy asked, and putting his lips to hers, he gave her a deep kiss that lasted for several seconds.

"Yes," Alex said. "That's a proper kiss, now, go away and let me get back to sleep."

"Yes, ma'am," Troy replied with a smile.

"Troy?"

"Yes?"

"I know you're looking for the man who killed your family, and also the ones who are blaming you for everything, and I understand why you're doing it." Alex stopped and put her hand on Troy's cheek. "But, please, be careful. I would not want to see you killed."

Troy chuckled. "Well, you and I share that same wish."

CHAPTER TWENTY-FOUR

Alex lay there in her bed of straw, listening as Troy rode away. She was confused about her feelings with regard to Troy Elliot. She knew that he was holding up stagecoaches, and even though he was only taking small amounts of money and from Welles Fargo only, she worked for Welles Fargo. And since she knew that he was stealing from the company she worked for, the proper thing for her to do would be to tell the authorities where he could be found.

She couldn't do that, Troy supposedly was wanted for murder, one of his victims being her father. But he had sworn to her that he was totally innocent of that, and she believed him.

Alex did not go back to sleep but lay in the straw while discordant thoughts tumbled through her mind. Then, when bars of sunlight began streaming in through the cracks between the boards of the barn, she decided it was time to get up.

When Alex stepped into the house, she heard Jenny in the kitchen. "Well, I see you've got an early start this morning," Alex said. "But then, as I remember my own days here, I know that this is routine for you, isn't it?"

"Oh, yes, of course," Jenny said. "Well, coffee's on and breakfast will be ready soon."

"Thanks," Alex said. "Coffee sounds awfully good right now."

"Also, Papa has an important message for Mr. Coburn," Jenny said. "It's awfully mysterious. Do you have any idea what it might be about?"

"I haven't the foggiest notion," Alex said.

"Me neither," Jenny said. "And Papa won't even let me see it. Will you tell me what it is when you get it? I'm dying of curiosity."

Alex laughed. "If it's a sealed message, the chances are that I won't know what it's about either."

"Oooh," Jenny said in exasperation. "That's not fair. People should know better than to send secret messages. They should know that it just makes other people curious. Doesn't it make you mad?"

"You'll learn to live with it as you get older," Alex said. "In the meantime, that coffee is smelling awfully good. Let's get some of it, shall we?"

* * *

The sheriff was waiting at the Wells Fargo depot in Canyonville when Alex returned. She greeted him. "What are you doing here?" she asked the sheriff, curious as to why he might be here.

"Alex, would you mind stepping into John's office for a moment?" he replied, evading her question.

"Sure, I'll be there soon as I get the stage unloaded."

"I'll take care of that, Alex," John Coburn said gravely. "I think you'd better go with the sheriff."

"All right," Alex said, her bewilderment growing now,

because both men were acting so strangely. "Oh, here's a message that I'm supposed to deliver to you personally," she added, handing the sealed envelope to Coburn.

Coburn put the message in his pocket and saw to the unloading of the stage while Alex, still wondering what was going on, followed the sheriff into the office.

"I'm afraid I've got some bad news for you, girl," the sheriff said as they stepped behind the partition that separated Coburn's office from the rest of the depot.

"What type of bad news?" Alex asked. Suddenly, she gasped and put her hand to her mouth. "Troy hasn't been killed?"

"Troy?" the sheriff asked in sudden surprise. Alex realized almost at once that she had made a blunder and she attempted to cover it up. "It's just that I ...I don't want anything to happen to him before justice is served."

"Oh," the sheriff said as if understanding, though still eyeing her suspiciously. "No, I'm afraid this is about your friend."

"My friend?"

"The girl who came to visit you. What was her name?"

"Oh, you mean Hannah MacDonald," Alex said. "Why, what about Hannah, did she…" Alex suddenly stopped in mid-sentence. "Did you ask what *was* her name?"

"Yes," the sheriff said. He cleared his throat nervously. "I'm sorry, Alex, but your friend Hannah is dead."

"Dead? But how? What happened?"

"It appears that she was murdered," the sheriff said. "She was found this mornin' with a pillow over her face. The doc says she was smothered."

"My God!" Alex cried, her mind reeling. "I don't understand. I don't understand it at all. Who would murder her? Unless it was the work of some fiend. Was she molested?"

"No," the sheriff said, wishing he were somewhere else. "She was lyin' peacefully in her bed. Only the pillow over her face and the blue color of her skin showed any signs of foul play."

"Was she robbed?"

"We can't be sure until you check the room thoroughly," the sheriff said, "but from the looks of it, I would say no. There is money in her purse, nearly one hundred dollars, in fact. And from the footprints it looks like someone just walked in, did it, and walked out."

"Footprints?" Alex was weeping now, and the sheriff shifted awkwardly from one foot to the other.

"Yes," he replied. "Whoever did it had been out in the mud last night. His tracks lead from his room to the bathroom, then to your apartment. Once in the apartment they wander a bit on your sittin' room carpet, though not as if he was searchin' for something to steal, more like he was tryin' to find his way into the bedroom. There the tracks go right to the bed and then come straight back."

"You say they came from his room? Then you know who did it."

"Not exactly," the sheriff answered. "But we have a pretty good idea."

"Who?"

"It was either a man named Armstrong, or someone called the Texas Kid. Have you ever heard of them?"

"No," Alex said. "I don't think I have. Why?"

"Well, since there was no robbery, and no rape—uh, excuse the language, Alex—then there can be only one motive."

"What would that be?"

"The killer thought it was you in the bed, and he set out to kill you."

"But why?" Alex asked, wide-eyed. "Why would anyone want to kill me?"

"I was hopin' you might know that."

"No, Sheriff, I don't," Alex said. "I'm sorry, but I'm afraid I can't help you at all."

"Well, I guess we just got us another one of them mysteries," the sheriff said easily.

"Where is Hannah now?"

"She's down at the undertaker's," the sheriff said. "I found a man's name in her purse, a fella named Denis Kennedy. We sent him a wire and he wired back that he's comin' in on the Midnight Flyer. I guess he'll be here on the afternoon stage tomorrow."

"He'll probably be here earlier than that," Alex said. "If I know Denis, he'll hire a team."

"Then you know him?"

"Yes. He is...was," she corrected herself, "Hannah's fiancé."

"I see," the sheriff said. "Well, it can't be a pleasant trip in front of him then, can it?"

"Sheriff, I think I'll go to my room now if you don't need me anymore."

"No, go right ahead," the sheriff said. "I'm sorry I've greeted you with such sad news. But seein' as how we got a good idea of who done it, you can at least comfort yourself with the knowledge that he'll pay for it."

"Yes," Alex said with a sigh of resignation. "Though I've learned that's scarce comfort."

Alex left by the back door of the office and walked through the alleyway toward the hotel. She felt sick at heart over the senseless death of Hannah, and a nagging sense of bewilderment, as she wondered why anyone would do such a thing.

Shortly after Alex left the office, John Coburn finished with the passengers and came back to talk to her. He found the sheriff still there, but Alex was gone.

"Where did she go?" John asked.

"Back to her place," the sheriff said. "She was upset by the news. I guess she just wants to be alone for a while."

"I guess you're right," John said. "Anyway, we've plenty of time tomorrow to discuss this money shipment."

"Money shipment?"

"Over one hundred thousand dollars," Coburn said. He held up the message Alex had given him. "That's what this letter was about. Wells Fargo is transferring that money to the bank here, to provide funds for the railroad. There'll be a special stage run tomorrow."

"I see," the sheriff said. He took the note and looked at it, and as he was studying it, Grayson Thornbury came through the front door.

"Where's Alex?" Grayson asked anxiously.

"She went to her room," the sheriff said. "She was pretty upset by what happened to her friend."

"And well she should be," Grayson said. "I only just heard of it myself, having just returned from the North. My God, Sheriff, do you have any idea who might have done such a thing?"

"We've got a damn good idea," the sheriff said. "It was either a fella named Armstrong, or another loud-mouthed fool who calls himself the Texas Kid."

"What?" Grayson asked, visibly shaken by the news.

"It has to be them," the sheriff said, noticing Grayson's reaction. "They stayed at the hotel last night and muddy footprints lead from their room to the girl's room. Say, look here, Grayson. You act as if you know those fellas."

"I do," Grayson said.

"You do? Well say, this is a fine break. Where do those scoundrels hang out? I'll get a posse out and we'll go get them!"

"I don't know," Grayson said. "I don't know them that well."

"But you do know them by sight?"

"Yes."

"At least we'll have another means of identification," the sheriff said. "Sam, Donnie, and the clerk at the hotel can also recognize them. We shouldn't have too much trouble."

"Sheriff, in the meantime I've got to make arrangements about this," John said, reaching for the note. "I want to go over the details with Alex first, but I'm certain she'll want an armed escort. Perhaps you can help us there."

"Yes, of course," the sheriff said, handing the note back to Coburn. But just as Coburn reached for the note the sheriff drew it back. "Wait a minute," he said. "Coburn, there's somethin' been botherin' me for the last few minutes."

"What?"

"It's about the girl, Alex. Are you sure you want her to drive that special coach?"

"Yes, of course. Sheriff, I must admit that even I had my doubts at first, but Alex has long since put those doubts to rest. She's the best driver on the route, perhaps on the whole line. If there's a special coach, then the policy is to let the best driver take it, and that would be Alex."

"No, you don't understand," the sheriff said. "I'm not criticizin' her driving. It's somethin' else"

"What else?"

"I can't quite put my finger on it," the sheriff said. "But it was somethin' she said a while ago. Somethin' about Troy Elliot. She acted real upset when she thought I was talkin' about Elliot instead of her friend from Denver."

"What are you getting at, Sheriff?" Coburn asked.

"Let me think out loud for a minute, will you?"

"Go on, Sheriff," Grayson said to join the conversation and thus be included in any information which might be forthcoming. "What are you thinking about?"

"Have you noticed that of all the stages that have been robbed, not one time has she been hit?"

"Well, yes, you can't help but notice that," Coburn said. "She's been very lucky."

"Luck may have nothin' to do with it," the sheriff said. He looked at Thornbury. "You've been spendin' quite a bit of time with her, Grayson. Answer me this and answer it truthfully. Could it be that she's in cahoots with this Troy Elliot character?"

"Sheriff, you don't know what you're saying," Coburn protested quickly. "You don't know how she hates the man who killed her father."

"That's just it, John," Grayson said quietly. "She doesn't think Elliot killed her father."

"What? How can she not think that? My God, you saw it happen. Didn't you tell her?"

"Sure, I told her," Grayson said. "But it didn't convince her. She believes that someone else did it. She thinks Troy Elliot has been made to suffer the blame."

"Then that confirms it," the sheriff said. "Coburn, you can't let her drive the special stage tomorrow. Don't you see? If she's involved with Troy Elliot, all she has to do is tell him that she's bringin' in over a hundred thousand dollars, and he'll hit it. It's pure and simple."

"Then that leaves me between the rock and the hard place," Coburn said quietly. "Hal is just too damn undependable. But I don't guess I have any choice."

"Maybe you do," Grayson said.

"How?"

"Why don't you send Hal on the special coach, complete with armed escorts and everything, but leave the money in Medford?"

"I don't get it. What will that accomplish?"

"It's simple. Since Hal is taking the special coach, you'll have to send Alex on into Medford with the regular coach run. Have the money come back here on her coach."

"What? Are you kidding? You expect me to ship over a hundred thousand dollars without any precautions at all?"

"But that is your best precaution," Grayson said. "Don't you see? Not even Alex will realize that the money is in the normal shipping pouches. That way she can't get word through to anyone."

"He may have a point there, Coburn," the sheriff put in quickly. "And what better way to protect the money than to let Alex bring it in? After all, she hasn't been robbed yet. We could sneak the money in before anyone knew it was comin'."

"I don't know," Coburn said doubtfully. "Maybe you're right. But I must confess to feeling awfully uneasy at sending over one hundred thousand dollars on an unprotected stage."

"Don't worry about it," Grayson said. "I assure you that this will be best for all concerned."

CHAPTER TWENTY-FIVE

"You fool! Just what the hell did you think you were doing? Didn't you know the muddy footprints would lead right back to your room?"

"I didn't think about that," Jasper said.

"You didn't think. Of course, you didn't think. And you, you're just as bad as he is," Grady charged, directing his wrath at Armstrong. Nate Curtis and Wayne Oliver were also there to hear Grady's angry comments.

"I swear to you, Grady, until you came in here with the news about that girl, I knew nothin' about it," Armstrong said.

"And why didn't you know anything about it? Your job was to keep an eye on him, wasn't it? Why did you let him drink in the first place?"

"He insisted on drinkin'. I'm just one man. There was little I could do to stop him."

"But you didn't have to go to sleep and let him go out and murder a girl. My God, something like that could have ruined all my plans. However, what is done is done, and it looks as if the event I've been waiting for is going to take place tomorrow anyway. So, with any luck we can take our money and then, gentlemen, and believe me I use the word gentlemen advisedly, we can terminate our relationship. You sicken me—all of you."

"What do you mean, take our money?" Jasper asked.

"Yeah, what's supposed to happen tomorrow?" Nate Curtis asked.

"Wells Fargo is transferring over a hundred thousand dollars by stagecoach from Medford to Canyonville," Grady said. "And we're going to rob that stage."

"What's the plan?"

"It's a simple plan," Grady said. "Tomorrow morning a special stage is going to go from Canyonville to Medford, pick up a locked box, and then, under armed guard, return to Canyonville."

"The plan can't be all that simple then," Curtis said. "The armed guards will make it dangerous won't it?"

"That's just it," Grady said. "We won't rob the stage that's being guarded."

"What? Why not?"

Grady smiled. "Because, my dear fellow thieves, the money won't be on that stage. It's simply a ruse. The money will be on the following stage, an ordinary Medford to Canyonville coach, driven by our friend Alex Pendleton, and guarded by no one."

"Are you positive about that?" Oliver asked. "That makes no sense at all. Why aren't they protecting the money?"

"Oh, they're protecting it," Grady replied.

"How?" Armstrong asked.

"By stealth," Grady said. "They figure that transporting the money in such a fashion will thwart any potential robber, because the robber won't be aware of the money's presence."

"Oh, yeah, I get it," Jasper said. "They're gonna surprise anyone who might try and rob the stage with the armed guards."

"Precisely," Grady said. "But the surprise will be on them." And on you, he added to himself.

Alex could only speculate about the special stage which left about an hour before she did the next morning. It had a shotgun guard on board, and four armed outriders going with it. There had been rumors for some time that the railroad would be transferring a rather large shipment of money from Medford to Canyonville, and Alex assumed this was to be that shipment. She also assumed that the secret message she carried the day before had something to do with that shipment, but she didn't dwell on it. She couldn't, as she had her own trip to prepare for. She was waiting outside the office when she saw Grayson approach.

"Good morning, Alex," he said, tipping his hat.

"Good morning, Grayson," Alex replied. "I thought you were going to get back to town yesterday."

"Yes," Grayson said. "I was going to return but unexpected business came up and I was delayed a little longer. I didn't return to town until this morning."

"Then you haven't heard about my friend, Hannah."

"Miss MacDonald? No, I haven't. What about her?"

"She was murdered night before last," Alex said. "It was an awful thing to happen. And here is the really frightening thing. She was sleeping in my bed while I was gone. I'm sure that whoever killed her, thought he was killing me."

"Alex, I'm terribly sorry to hear that," Grayson said with the proper amount of shock. He put his hand on her shoulder. "Listen, I know things haven't been the same with us of late, but perhaps you'll consider having dinner with me after you return from Medford?"

"Yes," Alex agreed. "Yes, I'll have dinner with you. But it will be the last time, Grayson, because I've something I feel I should tell you."

"Oh, I hate to hear you say it will be the last time," Grayson said, smiling ruefully. "But, whatever you decide, I shall honor and respect your wishes. I want only your happiness."

"Thank you, Grayson," Alex said.

"I must say, I already miss hearing you call me Gray, but so it goes. Do you have time for breakfast?"

"I've already eaten, thank you," Alex said. "I'm about to get underway. I'll see you when I return."

"I'll be looking forward to it," Grayson said. He touched the brim of his hat and took his leave, while Alex went inside to get the shipping orders from Coburn.

As she was taking care of the last-minute details prior to leaving, she suddenly thought of something Grayson had said. She looked up at John Coburn with a puzzled expression on her face. "How would Grayson Thornbury know I was going all the way to Medford this morning?"

"He found out yesterday afternoon. Mr. Thornbury has been very cooperative," John replied. "He helped the sheriff and me work out the special stage route and suggested that you take the regular coach run to Medford."

"Did you say yesterday afternoon? That can't be. He didn't return from Portland until this morning."

"Oh, no, he was here yesterday afternoon, don't you remember? Oh, wait a minute, I believe he came along right after you left. Yes, I can see why you wouldn't have thought he was here yesterday, if you didn't see him."

Or if he told me that he wasn't here, Alex thought. But the question in her mind was, why? Why had he lied to her? It couldn't be just to avoid her; in fact, it was he who continued to press the relationship between them. But, she decided, what difference does it make? After their dinner together, he would know exactly where he stands, and there will be no need for further discourse between the two of them.

The Canyonville to Medford run was the same route as the Canyonville to Summit Lake run as far as the Oak Grove way station. Beyond Oak Grove, the road forked, going west to Medford and east to Summit Lake. Therefore, the first part of the trip was like all the other trips Alex had been taking, and when she arrived at Oak Grove, she was greeted enthusiastically by Jenny.

"Hal came through this morning on a special stage," Jenny said. "I'll bet the armed stage was what the message was all about."

"It could be," Alex said, climbing down from the stage. "I've only got one passenger, and he's a through passenger for Summit Lake. Is there anyone here headed for Medford?"

"No," Jenny said. "Are you going to Medford?"

"Yes," Alex said. "Three more hours there, then three back to here."

"Good, then you'll be spending the night here on your way back," Jenny said, happily, "Only this time you won't have to sleep in the barn."

"Oh, but I enjoy it," Alex said remembering that she had seen Troy. "Really I do."

"Pooh, you're just saying that, I know. But I'm going to have a special place prepared for you by the time you come through tonight. Oh, I'm glad you'll be staying here. It's so nice to have someone to talk to."

Alex smiled at the eager young girl. How well she could relate to Jenny's desire for outside companionship, though she would have much preferred staying in the barn tonight.

"All right," Alex finally said. "I'll sleep in the house tonight."

"Oh, wonderful, we'll have a fine time, you'll see."

"Jenny, would you take care of the arrival details for me? I think I lost a locket the other night and I want to go have a look around for it."

"You lost a locket? Oh, how awful. I'll come and help you search," Jenny said anxiously.

"There's no need," Alex said quickly. "It was a very inexpensive locket, but I liked it. I'll just have a quick look and if it's not there I won't bother about it. You take care of things for me here and I'll be in shortly."

"All right," Jenny said, "if you're sure I can't help."

Alex gave Jenny the shipping orders to log in, then she went into the barn and climbed the ladder to the hayloft. She hadn't actually lost a locket, but it was a good excuse to visit the barn in the hope that Troy would be hiding in the little room he had built.

Troy wasn't there but Alex had prepared for that by writing a note before she left Canyonville, and now she opened the note and reread it before leaving it for him.

> Troy
>
> *I am taking the regular stage run to*
> *Medford and will be back through here*
> *tonight. I hope that I see you here. Alex*

Alex folded the note and propped it up against the oil lantern so that he couldn't miss it. Then she left the hayloft and returned to the main house.

"Did you find your locket?" Jenny asked.

"My locket?"

"Yes, the one you went to look for."

"Oh, uh, no, I didn't," Alex said. "It doesn't matter. As I said, it was inexpensive anyway." Alex took the shipping orders from Jenny. "Well, I've got a lot of miles to cover so I'd best be getting on my way. I'll see you tonight."

"I'll have a surprise for you when you return," Jenny promised.

"Good," Alex said. "I like surprises. Though the prospect of spending the night here talking to you is pleasant enough."

Jenny beamed under the compliment. She had resolved to turn the barn upside down if necessary, to find Alex's locket. That would be her surprise.

Alex pulled the team to a halt and set the brake, then climbed down from the stage and looked around. She was in Medford twenty minutes ahead of schedule, having driven harder in order to make a good impression on this, her first run to Medford. She walked into the depot and over to the station agent's cage. He was intently studying a time schedule, and he had a pencil stuck behind one ear. He looked up as Alex approached.

"Yes, miss, can I help you?"

"I'm Alex Pendleton."

"Yes?"

Alex realized then that the agent didn't know who she was. "I'm the driver of the stage that just came in," she said. "I'm here for shipping orders."

"Oh, oh, yes, I believe I was told that there would be a...lady...driver," the agent said, setting the word lady off from the rest of the sentence. "Well, it's good that you're here. I have six pouches for you. If you would sign here, please?" He pushed a form across the counter to her and took his pencil from behind his ear.

"Six? Isn't that a little unusual?"

"No, not too unusual," the agent said. "Why do you ask?"

"I've never carried more than one mail pouch and it was seldom full. And now I have six."

"Yes," the agent said. "Please sign this and let me get them aboard for you. I don't want to keep them any longer than I have to." The agent appeared uncomfortable.

"Why are you so nervous about them?" Alex asked. "What's in them?"

"What's in them? Why, I don't know," the agent said briskly. "I don't ask questions, and neither should you. Just sign here and I'll get them aboard."

"Very well," Alex said. "It's probably just old newspapers and circulars anyway. If it had been something important it would have gone on the special coach with the money."

"How did you know about the money?" the agent asked.

Alex smiled, then signed the form and slid it back to the agent. "I just guessed. Why else would they send a heavily guarded coach on a special trip?"

"You shouldn't guess about things that don't concern you." The agent took the form and put it on a spindle by the window. "Well, I'll just get these loaded now, and post a guard by them until you're ready to leave. Will you be pulling out soon?"

"Right away," Alex said. "Do I have any passengers?"

"One," the agent answered. "A man. I think he's back now, but he stepped across the street to get a bite to eat. You're early, you know."

"Yes," Alex said smugly, "I know."

"Oh, here comes your passenger now," the agent said. "You take care of him while I load these pouches."

Alex turned to look at the passenger and recognized him with a quick beat of joy. He raised his arms, and she ran into them.

"Oh, Denny, I am so sorry," Alex said as the two embraced. "It's all my fault. Hannah wanted to get her own room, and I insisted she stay with me."

"Don't blame yourself," Denis said. "I'm the one who asked her to come talk to you. If anyone is to blame, it would be me."

"How are her parents?"

"Naturally, everyone who knew Hannah is saddened," Denis said. He took a deep breath as he looked at the clothes Alex was wearing. "Are you really the driver on this stage?"

"I am," Alex said.

Denis smiled. "I have no doubt that I will be in good hands. I can attest to your ability to drive a team of horses." Then he sobered. "It seems friendship with me carries some sort of terrible curse."

"Don't think like that," Alex said as she headed toward the waiting coach. "You must ride on the seat with me, my dear friend. We have a lot to talk about."

"You mean it's all right for me to ride up there?"

"Sure," Alex said. "Get your bags on board and then climb on up, I'll be right behind you."

When Alex and Denis were settled into their seat, Denis noticed a large number of people standing around looking at them. "Alex," he whispered, "why are they looking at us?"

"They want to see if I can handle this team, I guess," Alex said easily.

"Doesn't that bother you?"

"No, not anymore. Generally, when I show them that

I can, their curiosity is satisfied." Alex untied the reins, released the brake, then snapped the whip over the heads of the six-horse hitch, and they were off. As they rolled through the streets of Medford, several people waved at them. A handful of kids and dogs kept pace beside them for a few blocks, but the kids soon tired and fell behind. The dogs, yelping and snapping excitedly at the whirling wheels, followed for a bit longer, but by the time the city limits were reached they, too, fell behind, so that the stage left town unescorted.

"I saw your aunt and uncle before I left Denver," Denis said. "They send you their regards."

"I must write to them," Alex said guiltily. They rode in silence for several moments, then Alex spoke again. "I was sorry to hear about Betsy. She was such a sweet person."

"Her death was a great personal tragedy for me," Denis said.

"I'm sure it was. Hannah said that you and Betsy were keeping company quite regularly."

"Alex, I don't know how to explain it," Denis said. "But there was something about Betsy…something almost mystical…that made our relationship a truly satisfying one."

"Denis, I'm glad," Alex said. "You're such a good person, and you have so much to offer, you shouldn't spend your life worrying about—" Alex's sentence was interrupted by the roar of a shotgun blast, and three riders suddenly appeared in front of the stage.

"Hold it!" the rider with the shotgun yelled. He leveled the gun at Alex, and she halted the team.

"Nate Curtis!" Alex gasped.

"So," Nate said, "we meet again. And Denis Kennedy! Fancy seein' you here."

"Nate Curtis and Wayne Oliver," Denis said. "I had

hoped to be able to pay the reward I offered for you by now."

"Well, look at it this way," Nate said. "With us still kickin', you're savin' money."

"What the hell is this, old home week?" Jasper asked. "Get on with it."

"Oh, excuse me," Nate said. "Allow me to introduce the Texas Kid."

"The Texas Kid!" Alex gasped. "You're the one who..."

"Killed Big Jeb Gibbs? Yeah, that's me," Jasper said proudly.

"No," Alex said coldly. "I was thinking of Hannah MacDonald."

Jasper grinned. "Yeah," he said. "Yeah, I killed her too. I like killin' women. So you'd better do like I say, little lady, or I'll kill you like I did her."

"You...you killed Hannah?" Denis asked in disbelief. "Why? What kind of a fiend are you?"

"I thought I was killin' this one," he said, pointing toward Alex. "But it don't matter all that much to me who it was. I like killin', and I'm the kind who could kill your ass like steppin' on a pissant," Jasper said. "Now, you just sit there like a good boy, and let the lady beside you do all the work. Miss, they tell me you're a good driver. You think you can take this stage down through that creek bed there?"

"Why would I want to do that?" Alex asked.

"'Cause it might keep you alive a little longer," Jasper said. "I'm gonna climb up on the top of the coach and keep this scatter gun about two inches away from your head. You're gonna follow your two friends down this here creek bed to a little camp we got set up."

"But what do you want with me?" Alex asked. "I'm not carrying any money."

The three road agents laughed.

"It's the truth!" Alex said. "I'm not carrying any money."

"You're carryin' over one hundred thousand dollars," Curtis said.

"No," Alex said, "you're mistaken. That money was sent on the armed coach. It went through here this morning."

"Open one of the pouches," Nate Curtis ordered.

"Open a mail pouch? Why?"

"Just open it."

Alex picked up a pouch from the footwell and unlaced the rawhide tie. When she looked inside, she saw several stacks of money, neatly bound in bank bands indicating the amount of each stack.

"I don't understand..." Alex faltered.

"You don't need to understand," Jasper said. "Grady figured it all out for us. All you gotta do is take this here stage down that creek bed like I told you."

Jasper rode up to the side of the stage, then climbed from his horse to the stage roof. He settled in comfortably and pointed the shotgun at Alex's head. "And try 'n' make it a nice gentle ride too, will you? I hate to have this scatter gun go off 'fore I'm ready."

Curtis and Oliver rode off the road and down the creek bed. It was narrow and twisting and full of rocks, but it was wide enough, and flat enough to allow the stage to pass, though it took all of Alex's skill to keep from breaking a wheel or axle, and to manipulate the stage through the close area.

Alex drove the stage through the creek bed for nearly an hour, when finally, it flattened out into an area that was obviously a camp site. Curtis and Oliver dismounted, led their horses to a tree, and tied them there.

"This'll do," Jasper said. "Now, you two, hop down."

"What are you going to do with us?" Alex asked.

"You'll see," Jasper said, grinning broadly. "Armstrong, you and Oliver," Jasper started, then he stopped and looked at Alex. "I'm sorry, you know these two galoots as Nate and Wayne, so I'll call them that to make you feel more at home."

"I know them as scoundrels and cowards," Alex said.

"You got spirit," Jasper said. "'I'm goin' to enjoy it when the time comes."

"Enjoy what?" Alex asked, fear creeping into her voice.

"Uh, uh," Jasper said. "That's my little surprise. Now, Nate and Wayne, get these two tied up to that tree there, then go get Grady 'n' Armstrong."

"There ain't no need for both of us to go after Grady 'n' Armstrong," Nate said. "I'll stay here."

"Are you afraid that I'll take the money and go?" Jasper asked.

"No, it's not that," Nate said. "It's just that I think we'd be better off if one of us stayed with you."

"Well, it's good you don't think I'll take the money," Jasper said, "'cause if I wanted to take it, I would, you know. And you couldn't do nothin' to stop me."

"I don't think you're goin' to take it," Nate repeated.

"Yeah? Well, I don't know. Maybe I will and maybe I won't. Whatever I decide, you won't have no say in it, you got that?"

"Yeah," Nate said, "I got it."

"Now, you, Wayne. You go get Grady 'n' Armstrong, 'n' you get back here quick. Tell 'em I'm thinkin' about takin' it all for myself. That'll get 'em here quick enough."

"Right," Wayne said. "What about these two?"

"What about 'em?"

"Grady said he didn't want anyone left alive."

"Well, Grady ain't runnin' this show right now, is he?" Jasper said. "And I aim to keep 'em alive for a while longer."

"Why?"

"I got my reasons," Jasper said. "You just fork your horse and ride."

Alex, who with Denis, was now tied to a tree, listened to the exchange with anger and anxiousness. Who was this mysterious Grady, and why did he want them killed? What reason did Jasper have for keeping them alive, and would he be able to do it? Her throat was dry, and her heart was pounding, but there was nothing she could do for the moment but worry and wait. And though she wasn't given to too much prayer, she found herself praying the same thing, over and over: *please, God, let Troy find us here.*

CHAPTER TWENTY-SIX

Troy Elliot moved through the dark shadows with the fluid grace of a cat and climbed the ladder to the hayloft. Then he pushed the bale of hay away from the opening and slipped inside. He lit a match, saw a white piece of paper propped against the lamp, then lit the lamp and read the note from Alex.

"She's late," a girl's voice said.

The sudden voice startled Troy so badly that he whirled and drew his gun all in one fluid motion. There, sitting off to the side with her knees drawn up and her arms wrapped around them, was Jenny Cameron.

"What are you doing here?" Troy asked, sheathing his gun.

"I'm waiting for you."

"Waiting for me? What do you mean waiting for me? How did you know I would be here?"

"I found this room while I was looking for Alex's locket," Jenny said. "And I found her note to you. So I knew you would be here. But she's late and I'm worried about her."

"Late? Late for what?"

Jenny explained that Alex had taken the stage run to Medford and was due back by seven.

"It's nearly ten o'clock and she hasn't shown up. I'm afraid something has happened to her."

"Maybe she decided to stay in Medford," Troy suggested.

"No. We had a rider stop to take supper with us. He left Medford after the stage did. He saw it pull out."

"Well, did he overtake the stage on the road?" Troy asked.

"He says he never saw a thing. Oh, Troy, I'm awfully worried about her. What if she went over the edge of the road or something? She could be lying in the bottom of some ravine somewhere, dead or dying. Please, go look for her!"

"Jenny, I have to be careful, you know that. I'll tell you what. If she doesn't turn up by tomorrow, you can notify the sheriff and he'll take a posse out for her. But I know Alex. She's just holed up somewhere for some reason."

"No," Jenny insisted. "Something's wrong, Troy, I know it. I can feel it inside. Please, you have to go look for her!"

Troy sighed, and looked at the note again.

"She left you a personal note," Jenny said. "That should be reason enough for you to go."

"Didn't anyone ever tell you it wasn't nice to read other people's mail?"

"It isn't mail," Jenny said. "It's a note, and notes are meant to be read by anyone who finds them."

"Have you told anyone about finding this place?" Troy asked.

"No, not a soul," Jenny replied.

"It doesn't really matter," Troy said. "If you found it, others can find it. I'll have to move my hiding place."

"Troy, please hurry, you must go look for Alex."

Troy saw the intensity in the girl's eyes and smiled. "All right," he said. "I'll find her. But I'm sure she's all right, so just don't you worry."

Jenny returned his smile. "I won't worry now," she said. "If you're going to look for her, everything will be all right, I know it will."

Troy flashed a big smile and turned to leave.

"Please," Jenny said satisfied now, "find her."

"I will," Troy promised. "By tomorrow morning everything will be fine."

Troy slid the bale of hay to one side and slipped through the opening, then crossed to the loft window, dropped down quietly to the ground, and ran into the shadows of the trees where he had left his horse.

The moon floated high and silver, slanting down through the trees with beams as visible as sun rays, though much softer and with less illumination. The illumination was enough, however, for Alex to see the two men who held her prisoner.

Nate Curtis walked over to the tree where Alex and Denis were tied. He was eating a piece of jerky.

"Are you hungry?" he asked.

"No," Alex said coldly, though in truth she realized that she was, having missed lunch, intending to make it up at dinner.

"Suit yourself. Do you remember the last time we met?" he asked.

"Do you think I could ever forget it?"

Nate laughed. "How about you, Kennedy, or do you go by Keller out here? Don't want anybody to know who you are?"

"You are an animal," Denis said through clenched teeth.

"Yeah, that's me all right. I'm an animal."

"Curtis, if you lay one hand on this woman, I'll kill you," Denis said.

"You'll what?" Nate asked, laughing so hard he could scarcely get the words out.

"I said I'll kill you," Denis said again, his words as cold as ice.

"You know, I honestly believe you mean it. Hey, Jasper, did you hear that?"

Jasper walked over to the tree. He too was eating beef jerky. Spittle drooled down his chin and across his scraggly beard. He made no attempt to wipe it off.

"What do you want to know if I heard?"

"Denis Kennedy, the dandiest dude of Denver, has threatened to kill me if I touch this girl here."

"Well, why don't you just do it and see what happens?" Jasper asked.

"I believe I will," Nate said. He walked over to Alex.

"Now just where is it that I can't touch her, dandy? Here?" Nate asked, putting his hands on her breasts.

"I'll kill you," Denis said. "As God is my witness, I'll kill you."

"We'll just see about that," Nate said. He stepped up to the tree where Alex was tied and planted his mouth over hers, trying to kiss her, but she bit his lip, bringing blood, and he jerked away.

"Give me a gun," Denis cried, struggling against his bonds. "Give me a gun and I'll kill you."

Nate laughed, then looked over at the Texas Kid. "I guess she don't want no kiss. At least she don't want none from me. Why don't you give it a try?"

"Maybe I'll give her a kiss just before I kill her."

"Are you goin' to kill her?"

"Yeah," Jasper said.

"Kill us both if you must," Denis said. "But before you do, give me a gun and a shot at this...animal."

Nate Curtis laughed. "Listen to him. He's crazy, ain't he?"

"I don't know," Jasper said slowly. "He might have a pretty good idea."

"What are you talkin' about?" Nate asked suspiciously.

"I think I'll just give him a gun and see what he can do with it."

"Are you crazy too? Why take a chance like that?"

"I like takin' chances," Jasper said. He walked over to the saddlebag of his horse and pulled out a belt and gun. "This belonged to my old man," he said, holding the gun out. "I took it off him myself, right after I killed him." Jasper opened the cylinder gate and began ejecting bullets. Finally, he spun the cylinder, squinted into the chambers, then put the gun back in the holster. "Untie him."

"Jasper, you aren't serious."

"I'm very serious," Jasper said. "Now untie him and have him strap this gun on."

"What if he gets lucky and kills me?"

"Then you'll just be dead."

"What if he turns the gun on you then?"

"He'll only have one bullet," Jasper said. "So, when he draws, he has to decide which one of us he wants to shoot. I think it'll be you, don't you?"

"I—I don't want any part of this," Nate said. "This is crazy."

"I said untie him," Jasper said coldly. "Do it now, or I'll kill you myself."

Nate measured the intent in Jasper's eyes and found it

sincere. With a final protest he untied Denis.

"Put this on," Jasper said, holding the holster out toward Denis.

Denis put the gun on, strapping it high on his waist.

"No," Jasper said. "Let that side hang low, you'll have a better reach for the gun."

"You don't have to give him lessons, for God's sake," Nate said, his voice betraying a growing nervousness.

"It's a single action pistol," Jasper went on, ignoring Nate's protests. "That means you have to pull the hammer the moment you draw the gun. When you get it level, its weight will cause the hammer to drop and it'll go off before you know it." Jasper took the gun out of the holster and turned the cylinder. "Go ahead and try it a couple of times. You got a few empty chambers to work with. Practice."

"Jasper, my God, what are you doin'?" Nate asked.

"I'm teachin' him how to be a gunfighter."

"But why?"

"I want him to kill you so I won't have to."

"Jasper, come on, this ain't funny," Nate said. "What are you goin' to do with him if he does kill me?"

"Then I'll have to kill him," Jasper said easily. He watched as Denis went through a few practices.

"Jasper, are you crazy?"

"Probably," Jasper answered. "All right, you're ready to go," Jasper said to Denis. "Now remember, you got only one bullet so you're gonna have to take your chance on which one of us you want to go for. If you kill him, I'll kill you. I don't intend to draw the first time, so if you decide you want to kill me you can probably get away with it. But remember that while you're killin' me, he'll be killin' you, then he'll be left alive. I think that makes it real interestin', don't you?"

"Let's get on with it," Denis said coolly. He turned to face Nate Curtis.

"Shoot him!" Nate said. "Draw your gun and shoot him. I'll give you another chance."

"Draw," Denis said.

"No, are you crazy?" Nate shouted.

"Draw!" Denis said again, shouting the word. Both men drew at the same time and the two shots sounded as one. When the smoke drifted away, Alex saw Nate standing there with a triumphant grin on his face. Then, slowly, the grin faded, and Nate toppled over. It was only then that she saw the spreading stain of dark on his shirt.

Denis looked at the smoking gun in his hand for a moment as if bewildered over what had just happened, then he tossed the gun toward Nate's body.

"Now, gunfighter," Jasper said flatly, almost bored. "How do you want it? You want me to give you another bullet and another chance, or should I just end it all for the two of you, quick and easy?"

"That won't be necessary, mister!" a man's voice suddenly called from the trees.

"Troy!" Alex cried. "Oh, thank God you've come."

Troy stepped out of the shadows and into the moonlit clearing. His gun was still in his holster, and when Jasper saw that he smiled broadly.

"So," Jasper said, almost happily, "I finally get to meet the famous Troy Elliot."

"That's me," Troy said. "And who might you be?"

"I'm the Texas Kid," Jasper said, stung by the apparent lack of recognition.

"That's a dumb name," Troy said. "No wonder I've never heard of it."

"What do you mean you've never heard of it? I'm the

Texas Kid. Why, I killed Big Jeb Gibbs!"

"I've never heard of him either, but we all gotta go sometime," Troy shrugged. "I guess it was just his time. Now it's yours."

Jasper's hand started for his gun, but Troy had his own out and booming before Jasper could completely clear leather. The gun slipped out of his hand and fell back into the holster, as the impact of the bullet sent Jasper back against a nearby tree stump where a coffeepot sat. Jasper tried to sit on the vacated stump but was too unsteady and slid off the stump and onto the ground.

"I wouldn't 'a thought it," Jasper said, unable to believe what had happened to him. "I wouldn't 'a thought you could beat me." His head fell forward and he died.

"Alex, are you all right?" Troy shouted now, running toward her. "Help me get her untied," he said to Denis.

"Just leave her there," another voice interrupted, "or this scatter gun will go off."

"It's Wayne," Denis said. "He's back."

"Yeah, I'm back," Wayne said, stepping into the clearing with the gun. "And I've got Armstrong and Grady with me. Come on out, Grady."

As all heads turned to look at the newcomer, Alex gasped. Stepping out into the clearing was Grayson Thornbury!

CHAPTER TWENTY-SEVEN

"So, you're Grady," Troy said flatly.

"Yes," Grayson said. "Grady is a name I used in my youth, and I found it useful to continue to use it in my extracurricular activities."

"I should have known it was you," Troy said. "Your mannerisms, your hands. But I never got a look at your face."

"No. I was outside, guarding the horses when your father was shot, then you were shot. I was surprised to hear that you were still alive. I couldn't take a chance on your mother and sister identifying me, so I killed them too. I regret that, but it was a necessity."

"I've killed the others who were there that day, and I've been looking for you ever since," Troy said.

"I know you have," Grayson said easily. "But you didn't know me, whereas I did know you, and that made it easy to avoid you. And I had the foresight to keep you alive. I figured I would have some use for you later on, and it has worked better than I ever could have imagined."

"Oh, then it was you," Alex said slowly. "You killed my father!"

"No," Grayson replied. "I didn't kill him. He did."

Grayson pointed at the still form of the Texas Kid. "But it's all academic now. Unfortunately, I'm going to have to kill the three of you. You, I'm afraid, are just an innocent victim, like the passengers on the first stage," he concluded, looking at Denis.

"I can tell by your language, sir, that you are an educated man," Denis said.

"Yes, I am. I'm a graduate of Yale, and I am a barrister."

"Then why have you entered a life of crime?" Denis asked, stalling for time.

"The answer is quite simple. Greed. This is a growing country, and intelligent investments at the right time can make a man wealthy beyond imagination. I have the intelligence. Unfortunately, I do not have the funds to make the proper investments. I have seen fit to acquire those funds in this manner."

"I see," Denis said. "My name is Denis Kennedy. Perhaps you have heard of my father, Ephraim Kennedy?"

"Yes," Grayson said, "I have heard of him."

"Then you know he is a very wealthy man."

"So?"

"He's wealthy enough to make it worth your while if you set us free."

"How do I know you are who you say you are?"

"He is who he says he is, Grady. I know him," Wayne said. "I knew him back in Denver."

"If you won't let all of us go, kill the others, but spare me. My father will pay you handsomely."

"Tsk, tsk, Mr. Kennedy," Grayson said. "It appears that you are not a man to be trusted. No, I'm afraid that what you propose is quite out of the question."

"No, you must listen to me!" Denis said. "Please, I beg of you, for God's sake, spare my life! Kill the others if you must, but spare me, spare me!"

As Denis begged for his life he fell to his knees and started crawling toward Wayne.

"Haw, look at 'im," Wayne said. "He hasn't changed a bit. He was just like this in Denver."

"Please," Denis begged. "Please, kill them, but spare me!"

"You mean you want me to kill the slut?" Wayne asked.

"Yes, yes, if you must."

"Then say it," Wayne said. "Say kill the slut."

"Please," Denis said, crawling all the way over to Wayne, and stopping just before him, "kill the slut."

"Naw, I think I'm goin' to…"

"Now, Troy, draw!" Denis yelled, lunging into Wayne and knocking him to the ground.

Troy, who had been looking for the chance he needed, drew his pistol and fired at Grayson, then whipped it over toward Wayne who from his position on the ground was trying to swing the shotgun around to shoot Denis. "Drop that shotgun or you'll die this instant," Troy barked,

"I'm droppin' it, I'm droppin' it," Wayne shouted, tossing the shotgun to one side.

Denis jumped up quickly and ran over to untie Alex. Troy, with his gun still in his hand, walked over and poked at Grayson with his foot, but Grayson was dead.

"Denis, you were magnificent," Alex said as Denis was untying her.

"I'll say you were," Troy agreed. "What kind of move was that?"

"That was called a tackle," Denis said. "It's used in a game called football."

"I've never heard of the game," Troy said.

"The colleges back East play it," Denis said.

"Well, all I can say is you must have been pretty good at it."

Denis laughed. "Good at it? I couldn't even make the team."

"What are we going to do with him?" Alex asked, pointing to Wayne.

"I'd like to kill him," Troy said. He cocked his pistol and pointed it at Wayne's head.

"No, no," Wayne screamed. "For God's sake, don't shoot."

Troy let the hammer back down slowly. "You give me one good reason why I shouldn't."

"I can get you off," Wayne said. "I know where all the money is hidden, and I can testify that it was Grayson and Jasper who killed the people in that first stage robbery."

"Troy, maybe this is your chance!" Alex said.

"I don't know," Troy said. "I've pulled a few jobs myself, remember? They aren't likely to forget that."

"What if you paid the money back?" Denis asked.

"I don't have all of the money. I've spent some of it to stay alive."

"Perhaps you would allow me to make up the difference," Denis suggested.

"Denis, you would do that?" Alex asked.

"I would."

"I don't know," Troy said. "I don't like to be beholden to anyone."

"Why not?" Denis asked simply. "I'm beholden to you for my very life. Surely my life is worth something?"

"Troy, don't be so stubborn," Alex said sharply. "You let Denis fix things with Wells Fargo so we can get married."

"Married?" Troy said, looking at her in surprise. "Who said anything about getting married?"

"I said it. You *are* going to marry me, aren't you?"

"Alex, you aren't supposed to ask me, I'm supposed to ask you."

"Who said?"

"Well, it's a man's job to ask the woman," Troy sputtered.

"Since when do I let things like that stand in my way?" Alex asked. "Driving a stage is a man's job, too, but that didn't stop me."

"She's got a point there," Denis said, laughing. "But if you don't want to take her up on it, I'd be willing to marry her."

"I didn't say I wasn't going to take her up on it," Troy said. "I just said it should be me doing the asking."

"Well?" Alex said.

"Well, what?"

"Well, ask me."

Troy looked at Alex and smiled. "Will you marry me, Alex?" he asked.

"I'll think about it," Alex said.

Troy kissed her, full on the lips, pulling her tightly to him. Finally, after several breathtaking moments, he let her go. "Well?"

"I...I need to think about it a little more," Alex said, her knees weak from the kiss.

Troy kissed her again, then released her. "Well?" he asked.

"Yes," Alex said. This time she kissed him. "A thousand times yes."

A LOOK AT: THE CROCKETTS': WESTERN SAGA ONE

SADDLE UP FOR A NON-STOP RIDE IN VOLUME ONE OF A NEW WESTERN SAGA – FROM THE MAN WHO BROUGHT YOU THE CHANEY BROTHERS WESTERN SERIES.

During the Civil War, they sought justice outside of the law, paying back every Yankee raid with one of their own. No man could stop them... no woman could resist them... and no Yankee stood a chance when Will and Gid Crockett rode into town.

After their parents are murdered by a band of marauding Yankees, Will and Gid Crockett join William Quantrill and his gang of bloodthirsty raiders to seek revenge on the attackers.

Someone's about to mess with the Crocketts', and that means someone's about to be messed with back. Will and Gid don't like getting shot at, especially by varmints who don't have skill enough to kill them.

The Crocketts': Western Saga 1 includes: Trail of Vengeance, Slaughter in Texas, Law of the Rope and The Town That Wouldn't Die.

AVAILABLE NOW ON KINDLE

ABOUT THE AUTHOR

Robert Vaughan sold his first book when he was 19. That was 57 years and nearly 500 books ago. He wrote the novelization for the mini series Andersonville. Vaughan wrote, produced, and appeared in the History Channel documentary Vietnam Homecoming.

His books have hit the NYT bestseller list seven times. He has won the Spur Award, the PORGIE Award (Best Paperback Original), the Western Fictioneers Lifetime Achievement Award, received the Readwest President's Award for Excellence in Western Fiction, is a member of the American Writers Hall of Fame and is a Pulitzer Prize nominee.

June 2021

CPSIA information can be obtained
at www.ICGtesting.com
Printed in the USA
LVHW041502120521
687230LV00011B/1590

9 781647 343569